The Take Over

A novel by Tonya Ridley

®

A Life Changing Book *in conjunction with* Power Play Media
Published by Life Changing Books
P. O. Box 423 Brandywine, MD 20613

This novel is a work of fiction. Any references to real people, events, establishments, or locales are intended only to give the fiction a sense of reality and authenticity. Other names, characters, and incidents occurring in the work are either the product of the author's imagination or are used fictitiously, as are those fictionalized events and incidents that involve real persons. Any character that happens to share the name of a person who is an acquaintance of the author, past or present, is purely coincidental and is in no way intended to be an actual account involving that person.

Cover design by Kevin Carr
Book design by Brian Holscher

Library of Congress Cataloging-in-Publication Data:

www.lifechangingbooks.net

ISBN 0-9741394-4-0

Dedication

I would like to dedicate this novel to everyone who has supported me in this endeavor.

Destiny,
Thanks so much for your support!
T. Ridley

introducing

Power Play
Media

in conjunction with

Life Changing Books

Acknowledgements

I thank God for giving me the courage and opportunity to complete this book. To my grandma Bethel Lane (RIP). Grandma, I know you are proud of your baby-girl. Mrs. Roberta Young (RIP), I miss you so much. Grandma Vandergriff (RIP). To my grandparents Frank and Ethel Ridley, RIP. You don't know how much I miss you. You always told me I was something special (I believe you).

I want to thank my mother Lena R. Ridley You told me I'd better keep writing, so I did. Thank you momma for being who you are. You have always made me think twice about things in my life, so I stand beside you forever, because you are what winner's look like. To my father Michael Ridley, thank you for the street-side of myself. I've learned a lot from you, and I hope I have taught you a few things as well. You know you are still the number one man in my life besides Joshua Washington. Josh, your big sister loves you to death. I don't know what I would do without you. To Grandma Ruth and Grandma Mary, you two ladies are the best. You are both still driving like hell, and smoking cigarettes a mile a minute. If it keeps you two going, keep it up and be happy. I love you ladies forever.

I'm so shocked that I'm writing acknowledgements, but when I went to the Supper Club, one of the best Black owned restaurants in Raleigh, I ran into Azarel, one of my favorite authors. Now, I'm calling her boss lady these days. Thank you Azarel for all the late night calls. You have been so patient with me. I am truly blessed to have met you and Leslie. You two are the best pit bulls in the book game.

To all of those who made this book possible, I thank you from the bottom of my heart. Kevin Carr, for the hot cover, my team of editors, Leslie G, Cheryl, Shannon, Jeri (Stink), Anita, and Leslie Allen. To the best publicist in the game, Nakea Murray, thanks for the publicity.

To Lisa and Emily, I know you got the street team covered, thanks. To Dinah Vinson, thank you for typing and making me smile, you helped me laugh when I needed to. To my auntie Joyce and Randy, thank you for everything. Auntie, thanks for the computer help, I couldn't have finished this novel without you.

To my brothers and best friends, Derwin Young and Petey Pablo. I couldn't ask for a better pair of men in my life. You both have been there through my up's and down's. You two give me the strength to always go on. Johnelle, I didn't forget you, so stop frowning and smile, wifey! To my cuz Rhonda and Antwan, thanks for always telling me to keep writing. But what happened? Shit happens?

Special shout out to Aunt Lisa, Aunt Judy, Reco, Antonio, Edward and Angel. Aunt Gwen, honey I know you gonna preach a piece on this book. To my cousin Latisha, thank you for helping me with my book. Earl (NC), Earl (NY), Chanel, Elijah, Marquez, Robin, Ashley, Othell, Daisha, Mya Ridley, Edna, and Donald. Thanks for always being there. To all my Tabron family in Philly, I'm coming to see you this time. To my sister, Andrea Parham and family, I love you all.

To all my closest friends, let's start with Carla – Girl we have been together thirty-five years, it has been long and hard but we still remain as close as sister's can be. Shemar, I love you. Nicky and Alexis, I love you both. Jackie D, we go way back, you understand me! To cuz Kim and Jackie, and I will always remember the good times. To Tara and Flip, me and Petey are keeping your name alive, love ya! To my home-girl, Jill Gatlin, say what's up to Jada and Jala. To Leslie and Alan Bland (D.C.) I love you! and Big Keisha, D.C.

To D.J. Smoove, I love you. Thank you for tolerating my mouth. I guess we will always be friends. Mrs. Lula Mae Griffin and family, thanks for being so nice to me over the years.

Mr. Aaron, maybe I can come see you fa-real now, thanks for everything. Natalie, please go back to the Sprint store. (We need you!)To my Gilmore family, don't we have the best memories? (Durham, Oakwood Avenue)

San Juanna and Monda, my Mexican connection. Karen and Danny – you two aren't gonna stop me from buying what I want (smile). Danny stop laughing so loud, Karen hang up that phone with Apples right now. To Malik at Millennium Fashions in Selma, NC. Thanks for looking out. To my NY Folks – P.I. you know you my people, we have been hanging since my hair school days. Special shout out to the Evans Family, Angela & Jr. Goodall.

Dr. Stephens and Angela, thanks for my visits. Pojay and J-mel, thanks for the cover it's hot. Ugo – thank you for everything, that you have done for me over the years. Big Texx, Bow-Boa, I see you coming! To Chanda Z and Shania, the Satterfield family and Shaka and Mikey – I love you all. The Jones Family (Apex), what's up G, Bennettsville, SC.? What's Up ? 1000 – Craig Mac in the Bahamas, Annetha and Mark.

To my other family, the Barretts. Ebony, Destiny, Mrs. Debra, I love you. My God-mother, Mrs. Jean, Madam, Mrs. Don Diva, Pearl, Queenie, or Queen Bee. Thanks for always keeping me straight, keep having the best damn parties Raleigh's ever seen. To Ms. Faye, what would Raleigh do without you? You are truly the woman of our "hip-hop" generation. To, my Godfather – Bruce Lightner – I pray you get better. Pat Wortham, Patricia Harris, Carolyn Jean Marshall, thank you for inspiring my hair career fifteen years ago.

To my Talk of the Town Hair Family, I don't even know where to start. Bryant, if this book is in your hand right now and you mad, put my shit down. Stop looking at the numbers in my phone. What's up "B"? Bell, stop laughing so damn loud, you know you got a client waiting on you, its Mrs. Eloise. Nicky, thank you so much for just being you, you always know when I need your help. Hannah, good luck on everything you do.

God bless you Pokey, Devon, Derrick, Soul, Big Shawn (RIP). To my people on lock down – you know I still think about you; Trick, Cube, Beefy, E-Man, Ghania Troy, Rahmel, Kiko, Jamaican Money, Skeet, T-Bone, and Pretty Dread, where are you? I miss you Jamaican Hardy, Jamaican Scareface, Mookie, Little Chris, Cotina McNair, Big Chuck, Black, Ty, Country, Block, and Pop.

If I have forgotten any one, blame it on my mind and not my heart. Send me a message on the message board at www.lifechangingbooks.net.

Post your comments about the book, or write to Tonya Ridley, 4501 New Bern Avenue, Suite 130, # 315, Raleigh, NC 27610-1550.

Chapter 1

Bang-Bang-Bang! "Oh shit, gun shots!" I screamed. My mom yanked me out of line at the Western Union, and shoved me to the floor. *Damn she's strong,* I thought. She laid across me like my great grandmomma's old stuffed quilt . . . heavy, old and ham scented. Hell, I couldn't move, better yet . . . breathe.

Just then, a mob gathered right outside the door. I lifted my head just enough to see a small pair of feet pointed in my direction. As several people inched toward the body, my heart slowed down hoping that the gunman had fled.

The fact that crowds of people blocked the doorway meant nothing to Ms. Faye. Boldly, her fifty-something year old petite body sprung from the floor and bo-guarded her way out the door, dead on the scene of the crime. "Somebody call the damn ambulance," she yelled.

"We already did," an older man responded frantically.

"That's just like North Carolina Police. They don't come when you need 'em." Ms. Faye lit her cigarette, as if she was watching a bootleg movie. As she thought about the shit, "Leslie...Kim, bring ya'll asses on out here. The police is on the way," she spoke in a strong southern accent. You know they gon' need witnesses. Hell, these crazy ass niggas wilin' out!"

As soon as Momma heard the first siren, she snatched me from the floor and dragged my ass out the Western Union like I stole somethin'. I felt sorry for the old crippled man she knocked down on the way out, but she meant business.

Outside the door, Ms. Faye stood bold as ever popping gum with her hands on her hips like she was invincible. While the bystanders rushed to save the young girl's life, Faye continued to yap. "Now, who would wanna shoot at a little girl," she yelled in between puffs. She looked for answers while one man began CPR.

Once outside the door, I wanted to throw up when I glanced at the young girl down and out on the sidewalk. Blood gushed from her head as her body squirmed to stay alive. Instantly, Momma positioned her hand quickly across my face trying to protect me, but from the opening in her fingers, I saw the bloody scene in three-

D. It was nasty, but a familiar site. "Damn," I mumbled. as my teeth grinded together uncontrollably.

The young teenager wore a cheerleading jacket with this big ass 'L' on the front. I wondered what it stood for, 'cause our high school, Enloe, started with the letter 'E'. I scratched my head trying to figure out if I'd ever seen her before, or why anyone would want to shoot a teenage girl. I'm sure she knew why someone was after her 'cause she was definitely the target; the way her sleeve was ripped, she was sho' nuf tryin' to get away.

Suddenly, three police cars dashed to the scene. People flew from the game room next door like crack-heads running for a free rock. Ms. Faye motioned for us to get in the car. She hated run-ins with the police. Her expression was so nonchalant, I didn't think she cared if the girl lived or not.

My mom on the other hand was scared as hell. She managed to throw my one hundred and forty-five pound ass in the back seat, and slam the door. She almost pulled the damn door handle off tryin' to get in.

"Damn, Leslie," Ms. Faye said to my mother, "I didn't know yo' stuck up ass could move that damn fast." Ms. Faye giggled trying to ease the tension. My momma ignored her and put the car in drive. She drove slow, scared the cops was gonna get us. Hell, we hadn't done nothin'. But, Momma couldn't help herself. She was a cross between prissy and straight stupid.

Momma peered over at Ms. Faye like a mental

patient needing Thorazine. Her eyes bulged three feet out of her head. She huffed. "What happened?" she finally asked.

Ms. Faye's mouth went a mile a minute. "I was so busy doin' what I do best, all I heard was gunshots. Shit, I almost thought I had a date with death. But hell I'm a hard bitch to kill," she said as she gave my mother a more serious look. "Besides, I ain't goin' out over another nigga's bullshit. 'Cause, that shit wasn't a mistake! Somebody meant to take her out."

I knew my momma was offended, but Faye and Momma been best friends for over fifteen years, so she accepted all of her—the good, the bad and the ugly. She probably gonna take her to the alter on Sunday anyway.

Ms. Faye continued. "I believe them damn shots came from the homeless park across the street. I don't know what could've caused her to get tore up like that, but I hope it was worth it."

My momma shot me one of those *you see what can happen out here in the streets look.* I turned my head slightly as Ms. Faye and my mom chatted about the incident all the way home; Ms. Faye doing most of the talkin'. Finally, we pulled up to the projects and dropped Ms. Faye's gossipin' ass off.

I been around this crazy shit all my life. While others grew up on riding bikes and playing in the streets, I was accustomed to loud foot-traffic at night, police sirens and plenty of gunfire. My momma tried to shield me from it, but with no luck. I wasn't as surprised as she was tonight to see somebody get blasted. Our hood was always bustling with dangerous activities. Either the fiends were out doing whatever it took to get a fix, or the drug dealers were trying to out-smart the police; who ironically paid close attention to our neighborhood. But even though they were always around, it didn't lower the murder rate. So far, for the year 1990, we've seen twelve people get put in the grave around our block. That was life in the hood-*our hood.* You win some, you lose some and others get *done.*

I'm just mad as hell 'cause I was tryin' to get my *ghetto child support check* from my trifling ass father. Big Mike was always comin' up short. The money probably wasn't in the Western Union 'cause that was our fifth time going there that week. We stalked the workers there so much they knew us by name. Big Mike was such a good liar. I don't know why he called to say it was there, if he knew it wasn't.

Still in all, my momma always forgave him. In return, she just wanted him to spend more time with me. Their bond had been tight. They were high school sweethearts and my momma's first *everything. We just wanted to be his first love too.*

See my mom and I never had much of anything. Although Big Mike's part-time donation was peanuts, we've always relied heavily on his $100 dollars a month payments. Living in the poorest section of Raleigh,

North Carolina on the South side did lessen our monthly rent, but we still sufferin'. My momma, known to her family and friends as Leslie, does everything she can to keep food on the table. A holy roller, she loves the Lord with all her heart, but for some reason the Lord provides the bare minimum. At first I thought it was a test, then I just stopped trying to figure out why we ended up this way.

My momma has held down her job at the Wonder Bread factory since I was in elementary school. Unfortunately, it doesn't pay much. She makes a measly $5.00 an hour. Now calculate that by thirty hours a week and see what you get. We got more bills, than money left over by the end of every month.

I don't sweat it, 'cause we've actually stepped up our game. When I was young momma would use lard to oil my body, now we're on Vaseline. We use to wash our clothes with lye soap, now we get to wash at the laundromat once a month. There were even times when my mother's coworkers would send me a bag of second hand clothes. And even though some were too small, those days were like Christmas! Now, I actually get a few new things once or twice a year.

What sticks with me the most-I specifically remember being laughed at in school a few years ago for wearing the same outfit three times in the same week. Forget about Gucci, and Guess, I was lucky to have fabric on my back. I never had the latest gear, even now.

Most of the time, I dress in denims and sweat-gear. But like momma taught me, I still feel good about myself. The saint that she is, she's always strived for me to walk the straight and narrow. I'm trying to hold on as long as I can, but the streets look promising more and more each day.

My mind keeps wondering how I can help momma fix a few things-money, problems and all. Tired of seeing her struggle, I've gotta make a few hard decisions. I'm a borderline bad g*irl about to go wild* and my neighborhood, Southgate, was just the place to make that happen.

Southgate was the shit and the place where I studied the game!. Everybody hung out *down at the bottom,* which sat on Proctor Drive, the last street at the end of the projects. That's where all the shit popped off. We had the hardest nose thugs in the triad, so nobody came over to our hood starting shit unless they wanted trouble.

Little did my mom know, I was starting at a young age planning how I would get paper. I plotted hard and always secretly found ways to hang out in the circle. We called it the circle because it was in the shape of a cul-de-sac. That's how I got tight with my crew, Chanel and Latisha. Even though we all kicked it, Chanel and I were the closest. She had been there for me, through good times and bad.

We did just about everything together-not only because she was my best friend, but our apartments set in the style of row houses, were right next door to each other. Not only did Chanel and I spend a lot of time together, but we knew each other so well, we knew what the other was thinking, before we said it.

Chanel and I have a lot in common. We're both virgins, and the slowest of our crew. Although the cherry hasn't been popped, we feelin' plenty of dudes; but neither of our momma's was having it. They were long time friends, and we were both only children, so they shared information about us often. Chanel felt the heat more than me, because all the guys chased her petite body and long wavy hair. I was sexy in my own way. Guys admired my shapely body more than my beauty. PHAT, I had been called on many occasions, never bothered me much. I knew it was a sign of admiration.

Our crew was well-known throughout the hood. We had the mini park and Mr. Jack's corner store on lock-down. Regularly, we raided Mr. Jack's store and copped everything from small candy to large items, like canned tuna and bologna. I figured I wouldn't burn in hell like Momma said we would, 'cause our family really needed the food. Besides, she had to be tired of eating all that bread she brought home from work. -especially with no meat.

As far as dating went, none of us were allowed. But that didn't stop us from being too damn grown. 'Cause whenever a brotha put his mack down, we were wit' it. The older boys in our hood thought they were our daddies anyway, 'cause they knew none of us had father figures in our lives.

At least Latisha had two brothers, but they were nothing nice to deal wit'. Her younger brother C-Man, jet black and *fine* as hell, was both business and pleasure. Forced to be a part of his brother's business, he ran the streets when he had to, but his first love was being a playa. He was approachable.

Her older brother Binky, on the other hand, was business and more business, but wasn't fine like his younger brother. Standing six foot one, and slim like Michael Jordan, he would fuck somebody up at the drop of a dime. Known as one of the biggest drug dealers in Raleigh, he had a brutal reputation to uphold. Many stories have been told about the ruthless things he's done to people, even his own flesh and blood. One time he gunned one of his runners down for not smoking his product. *What kind of stupid shit is that?* From then on, people were scared to spit his way. He even had some of Raleigh's Police Department on lock.

Even though the brothers were known to be ruthless, they loved us. We felt protected like a lioness protects her cubs; especially in the presence of Black Tye, Binky's right hand man. Black Tye was known to be wild and crazy. Most people thought he really had a mental problem by the way his body shook all the time. With a long scar across his left cheek, he stayed strapped all the time. We were secure *for sure*, because they ran the block.

I had the gift of gab, and would step to a nigga in a minute, so that always placed me first in leadership roles. Chanel reminded me daily that, 'I talked and analyzed shit, too damn much.' It only bothered her ass because she had a *goody two-shoe* reputation to uphold. She was the girlie girl of our crew. With a pretty deep mocha complexion, people often asked her stupid shit, like *does she have Indian in her family.* We laugh, but deep down inside Chanel doesn't care about beauty, she leaves the high maintenance to Latisha. Chanel cares more about school; always thinking about where she's going to college, and what's she's gonna do in life.

All three of our minds worked, but my shit stayed in over-drive. Yeah, I thought about the future, but I had also formulated a plan for now. In my momma's eyes, I was her rebellious little girl, but on the streets, I wanted to become ruthless. Tired of being busted, I decided to test the game . . . *the real game.* I decided, I'd break away from my all girl crew and take on the streets.

Having the heart to do things that boys did, I knew I could handle thug life. I was too young and dumb to be afraid of anything or anybody. It stayed in my head at an early age that I would be poor the rest of my life if I didn't do something quick. My momma never made me feel like I had to work, nor did she ever say anything, but I knew we were headed for the shelter, if we didn't get some help and fast. Deep down, I could see her frustration.

She was the oldest of twelve children, so the pressure was on for her to become a good role model for me and her siblings. Even though my mind yearned for the streets, her thoughts stayed on love. If it could be done, she would make things right sooner or later. But for now, she had the look in her eyes of sadness and defeat. I decided to fix it. I was going to make sure that when the weekend came around, I was gonna get my momma some money.

So I decided to holla at C-Man about some *work*. He was chillin' near his 300Z talking to some skeezer on a public pay phone. Walking up on him, I was real careful not to startle him. I didn't wanna get popped.

I stuck my head in front of his face. "What can I do for you to make some money?"

C-Man laughed and held up his index finger motioning for me to wait,, "Give me a minute, girl.". "Make sure you have that thang waitin' for me," he said to the girl on the line.

"Me and my mother aren't doing too good," I blurted out, as he hung up the phone.

"You have a good mom, Kim, don't do nothin' stupid."

C-Man didn't want to be responsible for putting me in the game. He dipped in it by force, only because of his brother. So grown-ass me, went for the person at the top . . . his brotha, *the big man*. We were always talking and bull-shitting when he came around, so I thought, why not ask Binky.

With me being only seventeen-years-old, he surprised me when he said that he could use me to start going across town. He told me we'd start in a couple of weeks. I thought that was the best thing I had heard all year. My new job was getting ready to start and I felt like me and momma were headed for the good life. I was excited about my new position, but wondered how I could hide it from my momma. I had two weeks to figure it out.

***

Chapter 2

My two weeks was up. When the day came for me to start my new job, you couldn't tell me shit. I had already planned to tell my mother that I was going to stay with my home girl Rhonda for the weekend. My crew knew that I wouldn't be around, because I let them know I was going to hang out with my girl from Lane Street. Rhonda wasn't from our hood.

She was about 5'4", pecan tan complexion, with light brown eyes and the freaky type that all the guys loved. Rhonda always wore her hair in a shabby ponytail because like me, she couldn't afford to go to the salon on a regular. That's why we were tight, 'cause she understood my struggle.

Rhonda was the second oldest of her mother's five children and had to make sacrifices for the younger ones.

Most of her clothes came from the 'second-hand' store, because her grandma didn't have much money left over from her welfare check that barely covered the bills.

She didn't like having to stay with her grandma, but had no choice since her momma left them there. That was the main reason why Rhonda was so grown for her age. Her cherry got popped at the ripe age of fourteen, and since then, her grandma couldn't slow her down.

Rhonda lived about ten minutes away, so it wasn't hard to line up everything between my mother and Rhonda's granny. I had it all mapped out. I would meet Binky, then head to Rhonda's house for the weekend. That afternoon Binky told me to meet him by the payphones outside of Mr. Jack's store.

As I stood waiting, big dreams of what I'd do with the money danced through my mind, Binky walked up on me. His eyes seemed to burn when he said, "Kim, I ain't for no games-this shit is real. Can you handle it?" he asked while clenching my shoulder. "Try this on," he said holding a cheerleader jacket.

I wasn't fuckin' girlie girl like that, so instantly I copped an attitude.

"Damn, you didn't say what's up or nothing." *He sure is about business,* I thought. Binky took a deep breath showing that he wasn't happy about putting up with my young ass. I didn't want to be fired on my first day, so I sucked it up and reached for the jacket. I frowned at the sight of the big 'L' sewed on the back. "If I'm gonna wear this shit, it could've at least been name brand."

"Be happy, you're co-captain of my sports team." He shot me a fake grin trying to ease our meeting. Little did he know, I'd watched him for years and never saw him smile.

I studied the jacket thoroughly. Flashbacks of the girl entered my mind. I opened my mouth to question Binky's connection to the young girl who got shot wearing a similar jacket, when he interrupted me. "You ready?"

I cut the small talk, and inquired about my package. Cash needed to be made. Three weeks had passed, and Big Mike and Western Union still hadn't come through, so I was more than ready. Binky looked me in my eyes. "We start with a soul!" He stroked his head. At first, I didn't know what the hell he was talkin' 'bout. But I got it. I was quick on my feet.

I felt him look through me. "Look, Kim, there are eight million mothafuckin' sad stories in this city, but I only care about one. Don't screw me over." He paused then grabbed me by my arm. "Ya hear me?"

"I got you."

"I got a lot of trust in you," he said sincerely. "I've watched you grow up over the few years. You look out for me-I look out for you. You got potential for the streets. Always be true to you and the hand that feeds you." I felt like one of his hoes. He continued, "You'll always have surprises in this game. Handle it !"

I shook my head letting him know that I had absorbed his every word. At that moment, my thoughts switched to how attractive Binky seemed. Although he wasn't physically the best looking thing on the block, I admired his deep, dark complexion and the way he took charge. My momma always said she wanted a man with ambition for herself and for me. Binky definitely got that.

When he said, "I like it," I snapped back to reality.

"Like what?" I asked.

"The hunger in your eyes. Trust me, you got what it takes."

I smiled like I'd won the big pot at bingo. *I'm a ride or die bitch. I'ma really show you how I get down.*

For the first time, I felt a real closeness to Binky, because he had faith in me. Nobody, other than my momma really believed in me. From school to my hood, everybody saw me as being just plain old Kim. For just once in life, I wanted to be viewed as the *girl with fly gear*, the smartest girl in the class or pull up in the neighborhood with a drop top Benz. I needed everybody's jaw to drop when my name was mentioned. Hell, I'll be excited just to have people look up to me. It was only day one and already Binky was doing great things in my life. *I gotta do good by him*, I thought.

"Binky, you can count on me," I said slightly nervous. For the first time, I realized this is real.

"Okay, Kim," he said, "let's work this hood." Binky

turned his back.

"What you doin'?" I asked curiously.

He faced me and handed me a piece of paper he'd folded inside a rubber band. "Never expose your money out in the open," he said, and turned to walk away. I watched Binky hop on top of the mailbox like our meeting was over. I gave the same head nod that I'd seen him give to his boys on several occasions then strutted down the hill. Curiosity was killing me. As soon as I was some-what out of sight, I unwrapped the paper from the rubber band to check my drop off spot. Shocked, I placed my hand over my heart. Wrapped inside the note was a crisp $50 dollar bill. I rubbed the money several times in between my palms. I was so excited, my first pay-off. It was official, *I'm on the damn payroll.* Plus, the added bonus was that my first drop off spot was familiar- *the Mini-Mart corner store* in Rhonda's neighborhood.

Out of nowhere, I caught a glimpse of an old, brown Cherokee with tinted windows rolled half-way down. They were headed in Binky's direction. When I spotted two black guns being held out the window, I panicked. I looked back to see Binky still sitting on top of the mailbox kicking it with Black Tye. Simultaneously, I shouted his name and gunshots were fired.

Binky reacted quickly. He slung his weapon from underneath his sweatshirt, and removed the safety latch. Before he could aim, three back to back shots blasted his way. I kneeled down low behind an abandoned car, fascinated by Binky's Scarface-like behavior. Black Tye got off a few shots, but never tried to take cover. I was impressed, the nigga acted like Robocop.

Binky finally took cover behind a huge trash cubicle, while I watched his back from afar. The corner had suddenly become a ghost town with the exception of the Cherokee stopped directly in front of Binky. A tall shooter swung open the door and hopped out like he was going in for the kill.

Binky popped up fearlessly, like dodging bullets was his specialty. He fired multiple shots toward the Cherokee, as the tall shooter raced back toward the truck. Binky took full advantage, and emptied his last bullet dead into the arm of the shocked gunman. Instantly, the truck scurried off leaning on two wheels.

By now, everyone knew what was going on and some came from their hiding spots. Out of nowhere, Tony, my neighbor who lived behind me, started shouting my name. He had to be calling me for my mother, because I didn't deal with him-period. He was lame. "Stop bringing fuckin' attention to me," I mumbled to myself. All I could do was turn around to answer him, so he would let my mother know I was safe. I kept one hand on the package and both eyes on my surroundings.

"What?" I yelled.

"Yo mama want you! She said she heard gun shots."

"I'm coming damn it!"

I felt like I'd smuggled fifty kilos of cocaine as I walked through the door. "Were those gun shots I heard?" Momma asked.

I hunched my shoulders. "If it was, it didn't bother me none. I gotta get ready for Rhonda's," I said playing like nothing happened.

"That's a nice jacket you got there," Momma said, checking out my jacket. "Where'd you get it?"

Ignoring her, I walked straight into my room.

"Girl, come back here," she shouted. "You got some boy spending money on you? You know, ain't nothing free," she yelled headed my way. "Besides, it look something like the jacket that young girl had on. You be careful!"

I nervously took the package from my pocket before *she* could suspect anything. As her footsteps grew closer, my heart raced. I shoved the small package in my smelly gym bag, just as she appeared at the door.

My expression changed instantly. "Mom, Latisha let me borrow the jacket. You worry too much," I stuttered slightly. "What did you need?"

"Rhonda's grandmother, Mrs. Jiles called. Her van broke down, so I told her I'd send you by cab."

"Now, you know we don't have that kinda money," I said.

"Kim, if I had an extra ten dollars, I sure wouldn't use it on cab fare. I'm calling my African friend, Mr. Prince-who owns a few cabs."

As soon as my mother turned to go make the call, I

grabbed hold of my gym bag. I figured it was time to get a good look at what was giving me strokes. Holding the brown, tightly wrapped pack, I peeled the edge just enough to get a sneak peek. I had heard enough about cocaine to know that this was probably the white powdery product that I now rubbed between my fingers. There was nothing to get bent out of shape about, 'cause it reminded me of *sugar*. I thought about how much money Binky really made off this small package before stuffing the pack back inside the bag.

As my mother's voice greeted the person on the phone, I followed her down the hall. My hope was that Mr. Prince would come quick because I didn't want to have to stick around the house too long. I was starting to feel crazy about how awful my luck was going. But I was determined to make this work.

As soon as I heard my mother confirm my ride, I mapped out my plan, and plopped down on our couch wrapped in plastic. We made small talk for the next twenty minutes until Mr. Prince called to say he was out front. While Momma was on the phone, I jetted to my room and stuffed the package in my over-night bag. Frowning, I grabbed the cheerleader jacket, remembering that Binky's guy would be looking for a girl in the jacket. Hurrying from my room, I landed a fat kiss on my mother's cheek and rushed out the door.

***

Chapter 3

Everybody was hanging on the porch, talking and playing cards, when the cab pulled up at Rhonda's spot. I hopped out, spoke to everyone and motioned for Rhonda to meet me on the sidewalk. She knew my day must have been rough by the way my curls were matted to my head. But surely she had no idea that I had witnessed Binky in a straight-up shoot-out. The first thing I told Rhonda was that I wanted to walk to the corner store because *Bloody Mary* came down a couple of hours earlier.

"Girl, at least you got a bloody visitor," she joked.

It took me a minute to realize what she meant. I knew Rhonda was a borderline ho, but I thought she at least made niggas strap up. "I'm saving my shit for the *right* nigga," I boasted.

"My brother said there's no such thing. You living in a fairly tale."

I thought there was something strange about her brother anyway. "Umh," I responded with sarcasm.

Although Rhonda was a boy lover, she did have street smarts. I hadn't told her about my package, but in due time-I knew her ass would be down, 'cause her house was perfect. The open door policy would allow me to come and go whenever we pleased and nobody would notice a thing.

We ran inside, spoke to Ms. Jiles, who sat at the card table talkin' shit, and headed toward Rhonda's tiny room. I kneeled to place my bag underneath Rhonda's bed, with hopes of everything still being there when we got back. Who could be sure, considering the hundreds of people in and out the house throughout the day. The minute Rhonda turned her back I grabbed my package and stuffed it into my pocket. Because we were in the hood, no one would be suspicious and notice the bulge beneath my jacket. Rhonda's way was action-packed, so no one cared anyway.

"Let's get to the store," I said anxiously.

We left the house and arrived at the spot within minutes. As Rhonda and I walked through the parking lot of the Mini-Mart, I searched for the client- a short, light-skinned guy with a long face and freckles. I didn't see anybody that resembled him, so I paced back and forth. Rhonda knew something was up when I didn't go in the store. She had a strange look on her face, but said nothing.

Soon, I became frustrated. When a gold Maxima zoomed by the store, it caught my attention instantly. The driver of the car slowed down after passing me standing on the corner. I knew Binky had told me the guy would be in a cab, but maybe he'd made a mistake. Once the guy pulled off, I decided to call Binky's house, hoping he would be back in the house.

Latisha answered the phone. I gave her small talk, before cutting her short to ask for her brother. "Where Binky at?" I asked.

"He here. Why bitch?" Latisha asked sarcastically.

I didn't take it personal 'cause she called everybody bitch. "I think some guy with New York license plates got his eye on Binky's spot. I'm sure he told you what went down earlier." I was lying, but shit, some guys wearing dark shades did pull up. And sure as hell, they were checking us out. So my grown-ass was soaking it all up.

Binky got on the phone pissed. I've never called his house and asked to speak to him, so he spoke in codes. "The dude not here yet," I stuttered.

"I'on know what you talkin' 'bout."

"You know."

"No the fuck I don't," Binky said, in a fiery tone. "Don't call back on this number!"

Damn, I got played. I stood in deep thought with my

hand on the phone. I wanted to ask Rhonda for 25 cents, so I could call back, but I'd probably get hung up on again. Before I could close my mouth from the embarrassment, a cab pulled into the store parking lot. Immediately, my hands got sweaty, and my heart pounded. The thought of what was about to happen had me wanting some of Black Tye's weed.

As I walked over to the cab, I was so nervous my knees shook; but I sucked it up. When the man with a red, high top philly and freckles allowed his eyes to meet mine, I knew he was the right guy. I walked right up to the window of the cab, said Binky's name and nothing else. When I dropped the package in his lap, I walked away feeling like the big dog on the block.

My first assignment, like school, had been done. As sick as it sounds, I was proud to do wrong. This was just the beginning of my criminal activities. That was too easy- like taking candy from a baby.

We went back to Rhonda's for the night and had a blast. I had to go ahead and tell her what went down, because she had seen me make the transaction. I filled her in, and told her I'd give her a little something whenever I came over her way to handle my business. "My only rule-never tell Binky that you know," I said. "He's real secretive about his business." Rhonda was a little scared, but she needed a little change too, so she obliged.

After getting back home, I was happy as hell to see

that my mother's car was finally working. My uncle had come over to fix it for her. Momma. And now he was faced down in the front seat, picking the dirt from the carpet. "Hey Momma," I said approaching the door.

"Kim, look. Uncle Bubba fixed the car. Now we don't have to depend on a soul to take us around." She had a smile as wide as our whole neighborhood. As she spoke, I thought about how I'd give her the money from my job. I slid my hand inside my pocket and held on tightly to the bill. "That's good, Mom," I said, in between my mother's gibberish. As soon as I could get a word in, I spoke. "This must be our lucky day 'cause I found something' we can use." I waited for her reaction. As soon as her interest was sparked, I yelled, "Bam!." I flashed the fifty -dollar bill in her face.

Her eyes lit up like the lights in Times Square. "Girl, where'd you get that money." She paused waiting for my explanation. "I hope you ain't into no funny business."

"Come on, Ma. I'm smarter than that."

"Then how'd you get it," she shot back quickly.

My stomach felt queasy. "I found it by the store near Rhonda's house. It was sitting there waiting for me to give it a home." We laughed together and embraced before my mother snatched the fifty from my hand.

"Thank you, Jesus," she said, raising her hands. "I can pay on the light bill and get a few groceries with this money."

She was so excited and it made me happy. In that

moment, I had accomplished more than any man had done for us in a long time. "I'm going up to Mr. Jack's store to meet Chanel and Latisha," I said, waving to my mom.

"Be careful," she yelled. "I'm a tough girl, other people need to be careful." She laughed like I was joking.

By the time I got up to the circle, Latisha and Chanel were on their second trip into the store. Like clockwork, we robbed Mr.Jack's store at least once a week. We took everything we wanted and kept a surplus for anyone in need. We were awful and knew it. Mr. Jack didn't deserve it, but this is how it works down South. We had a system in place. While Latisha served as the lookout, Chanel and me would go into the store and ask Mr. Jack for a brown paper bag. After he gave us the bags, we would fill them up, walk up to the counter, and give him forty cents each for all of the items in the bag. "You got your usual in the bag, girls," he would say.

We would shoot him a nod knowing that our bags were full of candy and any canned food that would fit. Although he caught us a couple of times, Mr. Jack never complained, so we started stealing bigger and better things. He's a push over. He kept lettin' us back in the store because he was known for helping anyone in need. *God knows me and my momma are in need.* The crazy part is, Mr. Jack has never said a word about it to anybody. That's why everyone loves him, because he can keep secrets, especially his own.

The Take Over

On the hush, it was neighborhood knowledge, Mr. Jack never said a word, but he is 'loaded'. He has owned his store for years, and is a heavy saver. What everyone doesn't know is that Mr. Jack is an aggressive investor. No one knows what he's investing in, not even his wife, Donna, *but she don't work anyway.* Most people have never even seen her.

We all knew Mr. Jack was paid because he let our mommas have a 'credit account' like he was running a major department store. They charge whatever they want, and pay Mr. Jack when they come across the money. He keeps this little green notebook, with their names in it, along with what they owe. He obviously don't need the money, but pretends to account for his merchandise.

Mr. Jack's store has everything from socks, to pigs feet, to bologna and eggs. You'll always find friends of Mr. Jacks in the store playing checkers all the time, laughing and lying about who's winning and who's cheating. Then you got the free-loaders leaning on his shoulder crying about their problems.

As I walked in the door, I thought about not grabbing the paper bag Mr. Jack held before me. I thought about all the good he has done, and the big grin he displayed in front of me. Mr. Jack liked the young girls, especially me, because I was 'thick' for my age. My big boobs, don't match my seven-teen year old body. But that doesn't bother Mr. Jack, especially since they started dancing as I spoke to him. "How you doin', Mr. Jack?" I asked, opening the brown bag.

"Just fine, Kim," he said. I shot him a smile that would melt anyone's heart. My 5'7" height made me look like a twenty-something year old. People thinking that I'm older is just what I wanted. I kept my hair pressed and curled most of the time, because momma insisted that it stay that way, and I sported the most fashionable hand-me downs my momma could find. Just because we were poor didn't mean we had to look it.

I got to the register, paid Mr. Jack, and walked out with my usual bag full of goods. After I left the store, I knew I had to ditch my girls because I had other plans. Hanging out smuggling candy was becoming child's play to me. Money was my new partner in crime. I had to keep everything on the down low. *Latisha can't find out that I'm slinging for her brother*, I thought.

I called Rhonda back and told her I would be on my way as soon as I got my next assignment. I reminded her not to forget to tell her grandmother I was staying the night again.

Rhonda knew what was up, so my plan was in place, and it was time for me to search for Binky in the circle. I couldn't wait to find out when he would be ready for me again. When I reached the circle, he wasn't there. I was upset. He had told me to come around 5:30pm or 6:00pm. Binky was known to be real when it came to time. "Be on the time," he always preached. You never heard of him getting fucked over or snagged, so I figured he'd show up.

After fifteen minutes or so, I felt my deal was about to go sour; still a no-show for Binky. I decided to keep on up to the store from the circle and hit Mr. Jack one more time before I headed home to tell my momma that something came up with Rhonda's grandma.

As I got closer to the store, I spotted Binky on the row of pay phones wearing a red bandana and an eight ball jacket. I got extra happy when I got close to him. "So you changed your clothes, huh?" I said.

He motioned for me to be quiet. I obliged and zipped my mouth tight. After he got off the phone, he told me that he hadn't forgotten about me; he just needed to put a plan in place to handle the fools who disrespected him earlier.

"Yeah, what was that all about?" I asked.

"It's the name of the game."

"What is?" I still didn't understand. I hoped niggas wouldn't just pull up and start shooting at me on my runs.

"Jealousy," he said with a frown. "There's a drout right now. Niggas broke. So anything goes."

"We gon' get'em back, right?" I could tell he liked what I said.

"Yeah, we gonna lay low til' the time is right."

I stood waiting on him to give me directions as to what to do next, when up walked Ray-Ray, with a sneaky look on his face. Ray-Ray's real name was Ray, but he stuttered all the damn time so people started calling him Ray-Ray to imitate the way he talked.

"*Ray-Ray, what the fuck you doin' up here right now, I told you to check out that truck from earlier." Binky's face tightened. "You come strollin up here like you don't have nothin' to do!"* Before I could blink my eyes, all I could see was blood gushing from Ray-Ray's head.

"Nigga, you don't call the mothafuckin' shots," Binky roared, swinging his favorite bat, a silver Louiville Slugger. "When I tell you to do somethin'- do it! I run this hood! You understand me Ray?"

Ray-Ray was embarrassed. He lay stretched out on the ground. "Okay, Binky, man, you didn't have to show out with Kim and everybody lookin'," he mumbled.

Binky checked his surroundings. "Let this be a lesson. I'm the man! And don't ever forget it, bitch ass nigga." Binky paused as if he was waiting for a response. "Ya follow me?" Binky kicked Ray-Ray twice as he let him go.

I couldn't believe he was asking somebody to respond after whipping the shit outta them. Besides, he loves that '*ya follow me bullshit*'.

Ray-Ray stumbled across the parking lot with blood dripping everywhere. Although no one else heard him, I was shocked when faintly Ray-Ray said, "*I won't forget this shit! " Now he ought to know not to fuck with Binky.*

I was somewhat scared at that point. Truly messing

up was not an option. Suddenly, he turned to me. "Meet me on the block at 6:30pm-*sharp*. And ,Kim," he said sternly, "lesson#1-you need a watch."

Shit, I didn't have a watch yet, but I sure as hell was gonna call my Grandma Mary Ann to send me one from D.C. I couldn't let Binky catch me without a watch after today, whether business went well or not. Plus, I learned another important lesson today. After seeing what happened to Ray-Ray, it was obvious that Binky expected me to do my job when he says to do it, and never take matters into my own hand. He didn't mention that I needed a bat, but I take good notes.

Binky was becoming a cross between the security I needed, and the brother I never had. Some nights, I'd think about what life would be like if I had an older brother, because then he could work, to help out around the house. Why were we chosen to be alone? Why doesn't Big Mike love me enough to be here?

I use to cry myself to sleep, just thinking about it. , but not anymore. I gotta be strong for my momma. We'll be straight when *I secure my spot in the game.* Enough thinking, I've gotta get with Binky and make this paper.

***

Chapter 4

My mother woke up the next morning with her voice on full blast. She screamed, "We've got money at the Western Union!" For some reason she believed that shit, but you know I didn't. I figured, either momma had lost it, or she thought I was stupid.

We drove down to the Western Union as fast as her piece of shit car would go. When we pulled onto Martin Street, Momma stopped right in the front of a no parking zone. She instructed me to hop out and take her I.D. with me. Most of the workers knew us by name, so I would have no problem either picking up the money, or getting embarrassed at the window.

"Come here, baby. I've got good news for you," Ruth said as soon as I opened the door. I smiled and Ruth replied by showing off her pearly whites.

"Where's your mom?"

"She's in the car. You need her?"

"Oh, no. But you might need her to help you carry this money outta here." Ruth caught me off guard. I wondered how much had come through. Ruth took a few minutes to approve the transaction. I watched her as she pulled the twenties from the stack. "One, two, three, four, five, six, seven," she counted aloud.

I was happy as a child with a new toy. Big Mike had really come through for us. I couldn't wait to see my mother's expression. As eager as I was to run to the car, I stopped and placed the money in my pocket. Binky's words rang in my ear- *never expose your money in the open.* I pushed the money into my pocket and ran toward the car. My mother smiled from ear to ear when she saw me coming.

I didn't give her a chance to ask about the money. I pressed the bills into her hand. "One hundred and forty big ones," I said.

"Well," she replied, trying to remain unmoved by the money.

"What you gonna do with the money, Momma?" I got right up in her face in an attempt to make her holler. I knew she was on cloud nine, but didn't want to show it.

"Well, we're moving on up . . . moving on up, to the East side, we finally got a piece of the pie." When I started singing the chorus to *The Jeffersons*, my momma cracked up laughing.

"Kim, you know all of our bills are paid for now. Lets splurge a little bit," she said with excitement. She looked at me for suggestions. "We could buy some plastic for our windows. That might stop the air from coming through during the winter."

"Momma, it's not winter anymore. It's April." We laughed. "What about some weed?" I joked. She punched me in the shoulder.

"That's not funny! What about some new towels and sheets?"

"Do something for you, Momma," I said in a more serious tone. "Get your nails and hair done. Get fly. " I touched her fingers to draw her attention toward her raggedy nails.

Our ride home was special; for the first time in life we were gettin' paper. Momma had enough money to hold her for a while, but I was waiting to see Binky to get paid for yesterday. As soon as we got home, I pulled a move that I know Binky wouldn't like; I called his house.

Binky answered the phone on the second ring. "Can I speak to Latisha?" I asked.

"No, see her tomorrow in the circle and don't forget the sizes for the team. Oh, and bring that slip with you," Binky said.

"Got it." I hung up. *This is shit gettin' easier by the day.*

***

The next day on the way home from school, I thought more and more about putting in work. Completing my first hustle got the best of me because I knew I wasn't going to stop, regardless of what anyone said now or later. I was so happy when we arrived at my stop.

When the school bus driver opened the doors, I saw Binky standing at the store talking on the phone. His pants hung well below his waist-line, and his Timberlands looked like they were missing a few strings. He motioned for me to come over, but I didn't want anyone to see me talking to him too much. Word on the streets was that the stick up boys wanted to take him out, so I started to walk pass. He stopped me anyway.

He told me something that would change my outlook on life at such an early age. Binky looked at me right in my eyes and said, "Mr. Jack died yesterday." Binky's eyes were so cold. My first thought was that he did it. He's the only person that I know who could murder somebody and act like nothin' ever happened.

"Kim, you gotta be strong," he said, raising my chin. "Losses happen. You still gotta be a trooper. Show your weakness at home," he said like a father schooling a child. "Ya follow me?"

"I got it."

Binky went on to tell me that Mr. Jack was talking junk while playing checkers with one of the locals. He started throwing up and went to the bathroom, and never came back. "His buddy went to the bathroom looking for him, calling out his name, *Jack, Jack, are you ok? No answer," Binky emphasized.* His buddy opened the door slowly and found Mr. Jack lying on the floor. He ran out of the bathroom, grabbed the phone, and called 911. People think he may have died from a massive heart attack. They're not sure.

"Why didn't I know about this," I said sadly.

"I'on know. Everybody knew. People been talking about it all over." Binky pointed to the store. "When the EMS got there, they said they couldn't get Mr. Jack's stretcher out 'cause people were cryin' and actin' all crazy."

I tried to hold my composure, so Binky would be proud. But hell, Mr. Jack was dead. That was the worst news I had heard in all my life. "So, how is his wife, Donna?" I asked trying to fight the tears.

"Word is-Donna don't have money to bury him."

"What!" Instantly, I thought, *I know I stole from him, but not that damn much.*

"They say, Ol' Donna was cheatin' on Mr. Jack and takin' all his paper. She ain't shit. Givin' that mans paper to another man."

Binky leaned back with his leg bent against the wall. It amazes me how he is always able to stay cool. "That's the type of bitch that needs to get smashed," he said chewing on his straw.

"We gotta help her bury Mr. Jack."

"Oh, we gon' all chip in with the funeral, but that bitch Donna ain't got shit comin' her way."

While Binky talked, I was thinking, *give me my fuckin' money.* No sooner than my thoughts ended, Binky slid me $200.00. I was on high.

Before I left, he told me to be ready on Friday again, because he had two people who were gonna meet me at that same spot.

It was on, because I knew that meant more paper. I was ready to go for what I knew.

As I walked home, all I could do was think about Mr. Jack and my next drop-off to the block. If he only knew the effect he left on us. Who else would show his kindness in the hood? Who would now be the center of our community? For that matter, who would run his store- *Donna*? She's never around. We barely even know what she looks like.

***

The weekend had come and I was ready for action again. I told my momma I was going to the next circle to hang out for a while. She said, "Fine be back before them street lights come on . . . ." I just cut her off from talking and said, "I know-You better have your ass in this house."

Momma looked at me and said, "Kim, you better stop cursing. You doing it too much."

"Oh, shit. I'm sorry," I said hugging her tightly. I caught myself *quick.* I had been smelling myself lately since my money was lookin' good. "I'm sorry, it won't happen again."

I strutted to my room thinking about my future earnings. Time would only tell how long Binky would really use me. I peeped around the corner to make sure the coast was clear, and shut my door. Hopefully, me and Binky won't have any problems along the way, I thought, opening my Pay Less shoe box. I spread the money over my worn carpet. I was sure the amount hadn't changed since this morning, but counting it had become a habit. Sixty-eight dollars was the total. "Damn, that's it," I mouthed, feeling motivated to work. I almost want to ask for a raise, but don't wanna fuck up this sweet deal. "Money- Money- Money," I chanted softly. It was definitely getting the best of me.

I shoved the box back in place ,and grabbed the smaller box that lay near the edge of my bed. When the top, toppled off, I couldn't help but pat myself on the back. A fresh pair of reebok classics was just what the doctor ordered.

Within minutes, I'd laced them up, and had my crew in sight. Everybody was outside telling lies; C-man, Chanel, Black Tye, and a few of Binky's insignificant flunkies. We all laughed at a tale one of Binky's chubby flunkies was telling. In the middle of the story he pointed to Black Tye making fun of him. Black Tye stared at the guy intensely. He had no idea what he was saying because his music played on the highest volume and was blasting through his walkman. Tye became even more jittery than normal, acting like he needed medication. Everyone hesitated, not knowing whether he was serious or not, 'cause Tye had managed to jump all over the flunkie, enclosing his neck between his rock-hard muscles.

Black Tye had been in and out of jail all of his life, so we didn't know whether this was a legitimate beef or play-time. When Tye jumped up dancing and singing everyone seemed to be amused, except Binky; he wasn't into music. In between the laughter, I motioned for Binky's attention. "Hey . . . "

Before I could get another word out, Binky said, "Kim, where's your motherfuckin' cheerleading jacket?"

"Shit, I didn't wear it up to the block because I ain't working today."

"How you know I'on got work for ya now?" You could tell he wasn't pleased by the way he scanned my body, "Kim, always think about work, and play later. *Everybody is disposable-even you.* Ya follow me?" Thankfully, I knew he didn't wanna kill me, 'cause that kinda comment could scare a nigga.

"That jacket gives me the creeps," I blurted out. Binky squinched his face like a rockwilder. I braced myself for his response. "You fuckin girls always worryin about clothes. Just wear the jacket, and do your job."

I saw some girl get shot-up with one of those on. You know anything 'bout that ?" I asked inquisitively.

"Kim, the jacket is so my folks can identify you. Now, either you gon' wear the jacket and make paper, or give it back and stay broke!"

I went straight back home and got my jacket. I made sure to check for the piece of paper I was supposed to have. When everything was in place, I headed back out the door, and up to the block to hook up with Binky. For the most part, I was excited about my business relationship with him, but personally I had become infatuated, and I couldn't figure out why.

When I reached the block he was still sitting on the steps, so I walked over and stood in front of him. Binky sat on the top stoop like he didn't have a care in the world. He stared straight ahead, as people in the neighborhood made sure to walk away from him as they approached his space. It could have been his firm, smooth mannerism, or the fact that Black Tye stood guarding him, with squinted eyes and an evil scowl on his face.

Although Binky rocked his presidential Rolex, and the gold chain around his neck that read 'Bink'; he didn't act like he cared about impressing anybody. He wasn't flashy. His goal was to make money.

I watched him closely from the corner of my eye. My intent was to be slick, but Binky is too sharp for that. He turned and looked me dead in my face. "Somethin' wrong?" he asked.

"I'm straight," I responded.

"Ya sure."

"Yep." My panties moistened a bit. I had to get myself together, and quick. The plan was to make money, not catch feelings for nobody, especially Binky. There was a reason why he didn't have a girl to call his own. Latisha told me that he played every girl he ever had. I wasn't about to be played. Plus, being a virgin in all, I was savin' my stuff for Mr. Cash. I wasn't about to end up like Momma. "Kim, c'mon and take a ride wit' me for sec." Binky grabbed Black Tye by his shoulder. "Stay here," he instructed.

Tye nodded his bald head in agreement, and continued to listen to his music.

"Where we goin'?" I asked.

"Don't ask so many questions. Be on my heels."

I shut up and moved," 'cause I wanted to become the female version of Black Tye, but smarter. Tye's loyalty was obviously an asset to Binky, but he wasn't the sharpest dude in the game. *It might mean a raise is coming my way.* Instantly, I said to him, "I need to be home before the street lights come on." He smirked . For once I saw a slight smile. "If you gon' run the streets, that's gotta change."

Binky's 1990 black Cadillac Deville was bangin'. The upholstery smelled like fresh lemons as I slid in the front seat. Hiding my excitement was a challenge, 'cause I ain't want it to seem like I wasn't used to nothin'. Immediately, I reached for the sound system, cause I knew he had some bomb music. Without delay, Binky slapped my hand from the knob.

"Damn . . . A sista . . . "

Binky cut me short. "Kim, this business." No music," he said. " Listen and learn".

Damn, I thought, *he is way too serious.*

We traveled to several blocks in the area. I could tell Binky had them on lock by the way people scattered when he rolled up. On the first two stops, Binky left me in the car for about five minutes, but on the third stop, I was surprised when he parked side-ways in the middle of the street and asked me to get out.

To what do I owe the honor, I thought. Within seconds, I had hopped out the car like I was a regular on the block, but stood out like a sore thumb. I wondered whether the two police cruisers that circled the street for third time, had even noticed me. They drove by slowly examining the hustle and bustle around us, especially focusing on the flashy cars. The intent was to deter the drug sales in the area. But like Binky, most of the people in the street pretended 5.0 didn't exist.

The commotion was out of control. Anyone else would've been terrified, but I just leaned back on the car like I'd been a rough neck for years. A shabby looking guy wearing a black trench coat walked up on us. "Dis what I got right here," he asked opening a box full of fake Rolex watches. Before I could answer, Binky back-handed the guy, and reached for his piece.

Just then, a large shadow came behind Binky. I motioned quickly to get his attention. Binky laughed at the fact that I thought I was protecting him. He introduced me to the big muscular dude named Roc. "My man right here ain't about hurting nobody," Binky said, patting him on the back.

Although huge, Roc seemed to be a teddy bear. "What up." I nodded.

"Get yo ass outta here," Roc motioned to the scared hustler. He playfully threw punches at the man in a child-like manner. Holding his head downward, the man stumbled away fast. "This yo lady, Bink?" Roc finally asked.

"Nada. Nigga, this my protégé. I wanted ya to meet her just in case she gotta come around sometime."

"She need protection, or she selling yo shit?"

"Who knows? Maybe both," Binky replied.

"Yo, right now, I got a .357, a nine, and a thirty-eight snub nose," Roc boasted.

"Damn," I mumbled.

"She good for now playa." Binky hit his fist together. "But she'll be back."

"Word," Roc replied, as he licked his thick lips. "Fine wit me. She easy on the eyes," he smirked. " I like thick girls; you know, somethin' to hold on to."

"Nigga, this ain't fa yo pleasure. This business! Ya

follow me?" Binky's face tightened and instantly Roc's silly attitude changed. My timing was perfect when I turned to walk away, 'cause Binky was all in Roc's grill. That nigga got a tasty mouth-full of Binky's spit.

Soon, we were back in the car, and rode in silence all the way to the last spot. I guess Binky needed silence while he calculated, and I was sizing up what I'd learned for the day. What I needed to figure out was how I would gain respect like Binky. Being his side-kick, wouldn't be easy, but I would demand respect too.

As we rode up slowly on Hargett Street, Binky pointed when he spotted Ray-Ray standing on the corner laughing with some skeezer, who was a cross between an albino and bright white. Ray-Ray's eyes scanned the top of her black mini-skirt down to the tip of her thigh-high plastic boot. His tongue could have nearly jumped out of his mouth the way he drooled over her. With his focus completely on the woman, he never saw us coming when Binky pulled directly in front of him.

Binky rolled down his window, and nodded for Ray to come to the car. "*Ray-Ray, what you doin', nigga. "Ya out here mackin' wit' these ugly bitches when you need to be takin' care of business?" Before Ray-Ray could answer, Binky was on his feet. Each step he took seemed to make the ground shake.*

"Nah, Bink. It ain't like that," Ray-Ray said surprised. "Man, she was just leaving! "

"Just leaving?" Binky gritted through his teeth. "She shouldn't have been here in the first place!

Ray-Ray, turned in an attempt to smooth things over, but it wasn't going well. With Binky standing over him, he stuttered as he assured his trick that they'd meet up later.

I laughed to myself when I heard the loud sound of Binky slapping the back of Ray-Ray's neck. "Nigga, you are a complete fuck-up," Binky shouted.

Even though Ray-Ray was embarrassed, I continued to laugh. *Fuck that stupid nigga,* I thought. Binky finally lightened up by laughing too. "Yo ignorant ass gon' fuck up the business for an ugly ho!" I started to laugh even harder when Ray and I made eye contact.

"Kim, you must think I'm some sucka ass nigga." Ray-Ray pointed at me like it was a death-wish. For some reason he hated me, and I hadn't done a damn thing to him. Binky had plenty of runners, and they all liked me. Ray-Ray seemed to make me the enemy.

Binky sped off, with both of us still laughing at Ray-Ray and his broke down ho! As we were riding down the street, Binky, gave me one of his infamous looks. "Kim, I know you won't do no crazy shit while takin' care of business. "

I felt all mushy inside, because Binky seemed to really trust me. I nestled back in the seat like he was my man. With my right hand, I turned the dial with ease, and smiled devilishly at Binky as *Fuck the Police* by NWA blasted through the system. He looked at me and just frowned.

Our last stop was near Rhonda's house. When Binky hopped out of the car, he walked pass a few cars until he reached a familiar looking car. It was the guys with the New York plates again. My neck stretched like a fuckin' slinky tryin' to be nosey. Although the Cressida was parked about ten yards from me, I behaved like a seeing-eye dog. The excitement in seeing those niggas again, had me going, especially the Jamaican guy with the dreads. His muscular build got me all wound up.

Binky didn't say a word until he and the driver of the Cressida walked away from the cars. They exchanged dap like they were old-time friends, and walked closer to where I sat. *My view was perfect.* The Jamaican was a little more flashy then Binky. You could tell he liked to spend money, by the gold and diamonds draped around his neck and clutched on his fingers. They talked for a few minutes in codes, while I tried my hand at reading lips. I couldn't make out a word, but damn sho tried.

I wanted to go to the pay phone and call Rhonda to tell her about the Jamaican, but I was too scared to make any sloppy moves. Luckily, after a few minutes of small talk, they both walked toward my side of the car. Neither of them said a word to me, but the look the Jamaican gave me was unexplainable. I turned my head as quick as possible. I didn't know whether he thought I was an associate, or Binky's girl. Either was fine with me. I wondered what that was all about, but didn't ask any questions.

Moments later, Binky was back in the car and silent again.

"He working with you?" I asked.

"Nah, he just another nigga in the streets needing some info."

"So, who does he work for?"

Binky ignored me. If I didn't know better, I'd think he was the CEO of a major organization the way he stayed in deep thought. It was fine with me though; It was 'like that' for me to be riding around with him, and I was enjoying every minute of it.

Right before we reached our block, we stopped by another store that I had never been to. I glanced at the store when we pulled to the front. Trying to count the iron bars got me so confused, I could barely make out the location of the front door. The store was so run down, it reminded me of a haunted shack.

"Kim get out."

Get out, I thought. "I'ma tough bitch, but hell you gotta be God himself to go up in there." I sighed. "Where's the package?" He kept looking straight ahead. I was beginning to learn what his silent stares meant.

"When ya se 'em, give 'em the package. Tell 'em Binky sent ya."

I didn't speak- I just fumbled around inside my pocket. Nervous, I jumped out of my seat and headed for the door. In my mind, I wondered when he had a chance to put the package in my jacket. I gotta watch his ass. That's the type of nigga, Ms. Faye said would slip a young girl like me a mickey.

Once inside, I asked the clerk for Johnny Dollar. A white man came out of the back, behind some curtains and said, "I'm Johnny. What can I help you with?"

Shocked, I hesitated. I expected a big, black, Barry White look-a-like. Instead, I got a wacked-out, Dick Van Dyke. I couldn't figure out why they called him Johnny Dollar 'cause he didn't look like he had two quarters to rub together. His tye-dyed t-shirt complimented his old ass flip flops. I quickly changed my focus, concentrating on the job I came to do.

I carefully removed the package while examining the room. Large brown boxes filled the junky space. Before I handed it over, I checked the corner ceilings for cameras. "Binky sent me," I said, as I handed it over. Johnny Dollar grinned like he was pleased with my performance. I turned to walk away. This job was so easy that I was ready to step up in the game.

I wanted this to be my permanent job when I got out of high school which wouldn't be too much longer. I got back in Binky's car, and immediately told him about my future plans.

"Girl, yo ass is learnin', but not fast enough."

"Why you say that?"

He shook his head. "Kim, I slipped that small

package in your jacket while we were riding. You didn't even feel it. You know why?"

"No."

"'Cause you ain't focused. You busy flossin'."

"It's not about funnin', its about staying outta jail. Don't let it happen to you again. Ya follow me?"

"I follow you," I repeated sarcastically. But to myself, I mouthed *don't try to test me mothafucka, I bet you won't ever get away with that shit again.*

Our next stop was home and the streetlights had about fifteen minutes to pop on. They came on every night around 7:30p.m. We stopped at my circle so I wouldn't have too far to walk. As we rode pass Mr. Jack's store, I asked Binky if he had helped Donna pay for the funeral yet.

He paused. "Yeah, I helped the bitch."

I was so happy to hear that. Stealing from such a good man had been on my conscious lately. Even though I was hard-nosed, I wanted to do something special to pay my respects, but couldn't think of anything as of yet.

"Binky, you goin' to the service."

"No doubt. Are you?"

"Yeah"

I'm gonna ask my mother if we're going. If she says no, I'm tryna go with you."

"Oh, hell nah . . . ," he said. "Not this time, Kim. It's not the right place. I need to show up alone. Naw me,I'm solo.

Oh, he don't want to be seen with me.

Later, he gonna wish he was in me. I smiled thinking about my plan working out.

As soon as Binky laced my hand with two 'C' notes, my mind raced. I ran fast, and called Chanel to run down our shopping plans. By the time we got off the phone, my eyes were as heavy as a truck load of concrete. It was settled. Friday, Chanel and I would shop for an outfit for the funeral and anything else my funds would buy.

***

Chapter 5

After a long day of learning the ropes with Binky, I needed some rest.

I could barely make out the sounds coming from our apartment, as I stuck my key in the worn hole. Instantly, the bottle of E&J sitting on the end table caught my attention. *Now, I know my momma ain't let Ms. Faye drink that shit up in our house; especially after all the lip she gives me.* I wanted to investigate, but hurried toward my room to hide the shopping bags full of clothes. Between the ruffling sounds coming from the bags and the moans coming from my momma's room, I was starting to hear things. After successfully hiding the bags, I yelled, "Momma." I got no response. *That's strange,* I thought.

Headed toward her bedroom door, the sound of

things falling to the floor had me wondering what was going on. I turned the knob and walked right in. When I saw him standing there, my jaw dropped two inches and hung open like a basketball hoop. At least he could have the decency to put some clothes on, instead of standing there butt naked with a pillow over his dick.

My momma moved slightly to the side to let him pass. I almost didn't recognize him, because it had been such a long time. But unfortunately for me, I was the spitting image of him. Standing six foot four, my father resembled a heavy-set, attractive wrestler, with curly black hair.

I backed away from the room without even shutting the door. My first instinct was to leave, but then I thought about it. Why should I run away from my damn home? We ain't seen this nigga in six months, and he up in here poking my momma. He needs to bounce.

I hurried to the kitchen and popped open a can of tuna. I was determined to make them uncomfortable, if and when they came into the living room. Between humming, whistling, and anything else I could think of, Big Mike appeared before me. He grinned like we were old friends. In return, I ignored his hefty ass.

"How you doin', Kim?" he asked.

"Same as always," I responded, mixing the mayo and pickles.

He tried his best to get me to look at him. "You know I miss you and your mother." His breathing intensified.

"Umgh."

"What does that mean?" he questioned.

"Not a thing."

"I see you've changed since I've been gone."

"I had to." I finally looked him dead in the face, and rolled my eyes as hard as I could. "We gotta survive. So I had to grow up."

"Kim, I know you're mad at me. But that doesn't excuse what you've gotten yourself into."

"What? I'm damn near grown."

Big Mike blurted out, "So you think dealing with Binky makes you grown." I nearly lost my breath. His words echoed in my head, over and over again. I started scraping the freshly made tuna into the trash, instead of on my plate. Luckily for me, my momma walked in, and Mike changed the subject.

I wanted to throw up when I saw him rub the lower part of her back. "Kim, at some point we need to talk," he said. "Your mother and I are headed out to talk about a few things. You and I need a moment a little later."

I gave my momma the look of death. But nothing could wipe the glow from her face. Big Mike had obviously given her the black two-piece set she sported. I said absolutely nothing as they headed for the door. I was on fire with this fat mothafucker. First, he had my mother camping out at the Western Union for no fuckin' reason, then he shows up acting like Prince Charming. Not to mention, over-stepping his boundaries with me.

Hell, the day I stop fuckin' with Binky, will be the same day he starts footin' the bills around here.

As soon as the door closed, my tears poured. Mixed feelings flooded my mind. My daddy was actually in the same house with me, and Momma seemed at peace. But, I hated him for leaving us. What was in D.C. that kept him away for so long? I headed straight for the phone. All I could do was call Rhonda and Chanel on three-way and tell them about this shit.

I called Chanel first. "Hello."

"What's up Pocahontas?"

"Nothing, Kim- just got home from the doctor's office."

"You been going to the doctors a lot lately," I said.

"Yeah, but I'm straight."

"Girl, you don't wanna know what just happened to me."

"Tell me," Chanel yelled.

"Oh, it ain't nothin' good. As a matter of fact, it's pretty bad."

"Spit it out," Chanel said impatiently.

First, I tried to click Rhonda in, but after hearing her line ring three times, I hung up. Chanel's patience dwindled real quick. "C'mon, girl, tell me."

"My dad is in town. And it looks like he might be staying here."

"Say it ain't so," Chanel screamed again. "Girl, you aught to be glad. I don't even know who my daddy is."

"Girl, I'm so . . . stressed. You still goin' to the funeral tomorrow, right?"

"You bet."

"Alright, I'll check you in the a.m," I said, pretending that everything was gonna be okay. But in all actuality, Big Mike coming back to town was a thorn in my side, and posed a potential problem for me financially. I wasn't quite sure how much he knew about Binky, or what was told to him. I slammed my head between my pillows hoping this was all a bad dream. I wanted to blink two times, and have my dad's black ass disappear; but I gave up, and called it a night. I needed to think on this new daddy bullshit, and how I'd make my drug deals work with him in town.

I already had it planned in my head that if he told my mother anything, I would deny the shit to the end. All I could hear my mother saying is, "Kim, I didn't raise you that way." And I wasn't ready for any of that right now. I wanted *money.* As usual, my mind worked overtime while I put my plan in action. I wasn't sure how long Big Mike would be here invading my space, but I sure as hell would stay out of his way. Instantly, I got up and set my clock for 5 a.m. I hopped back in bed and fell fast asleep within seconds.

***

The next morning like clockwork, I got up early, got everything I needed and started towards the door before my mom could talk to me. I was willing to bet money that if I'd gone in her room, I'd find my dad lying right next to her. *This happy family bullshit was working my nerves.*

School didn't start until 8 o'clock, but considering my grades lately, the extra study time wouldn't hurt. I crept into the living room careful not to make too much noise. I panicked at the sight of a huge figure lying on the couch. I started to move closer, when the familiar body turned slightly. *Momma definitely gotta start charging him rent,* I thought. With Big Mike on the couch, and Momma in her room, I was determined to be outta there.

***

As soon as the bell rang, I was ready to make my move. I stopped by Mr. Jack's store in hopes of grabbing a Gatorade, forgetting that the store hadn't re-opened yet. For sure- that 5 a.m. trick, hurt me more than it hurt my momma. And for once, I knew the answers during my history discussion today, but couldn't manage to lift my head to speak.

As I approached the next circle, I forgot about the tiredness, and put on my game face. "You got what I need," I asked Black-Tye. I bobbed my head back and forth like I had a beef to settle.

He laughed. "You ready to get your hustle on, huh?"

he asked, with the smell of weed on his breath.

"Damn right," I said with confidence.

I watched Black Tye push his piece inside his jeans. Now even though I knew Binky carried his buddy- good ol' Smith and Wesson, he concealed it. It was almost as if Black Tye was checking to make sure his piece was working. When cab twelve arrived, I was ready to go. "Lets do this, Kim," he said. "We gonna deliver the package to Johnny Dollar."

Shit, I knew he didn't need a gun for him. But, it felt good hearing the name Johnny Dollar. I had done a good job on my first meeting with him, so the second time around would be a breeze.

"Don't fuck up," Tye repeated twice in the cab.

"Shu . . . " I said, placing a finger over my lips.

He laughed hysterically. He always had a way of over-doing things. "The driver is the least of our worries. He's one of us."

Damn, I thought. This is some Mafia shit. I shot Tye a look of excitement. For some reason, he was more crazed than me. He wobbled his bulky frame back and forth in the seat, listening to his music. I see why Binky wanted to train me. He was rollin' with a bunch of fools. I was revved up and ready to put in work. I tried to see what Black Tye really thought about me, 'cause he didn't talk much. "If you want, I'll handle the transaction. You can stay in the car," I said.

Tye looked at me like I'd just smoked twelve blunts.

"How you gonna handle yourself, Kim? You got a gun? Better yet, do you got heart?"

I ignored him and held out my hand for the package. We sat right in front of Johnny Dollar's spot like two fools waiting to be spotted. Tye came from his daze, and greased my palm with the product.

"Stay here," I ordered, trying to be gangsta. Black Tye agreed at first, but suddenly swung open the door like the *Terminator* to follow me. I hurried boldly to the sidewalk trying to create some space between the two of us. I wanted him to know that I could handle myself.

Two steps from Johnny's door, I noticed a masked man running toward me. I had to think quick. I stuffed the package into my pants, and ducked simultaneously. Everything moved in slow motion. Black-Tye jumped from behind the cab and shot the nigga face first. His body squirmed on the ground as if he was fighting to stay alive.

Instantly, I moved in closer, trying to decide if I'd run for help. Then it clicked; this nigga wasn't worth being saved. He was trying to get me! Instead of fear, I became enraged and snatched the nine from Black Tye's hand. POW! I shot his ass again.

In shock, I couldn't move. Before I knew it, Tye had grabbed me by the collar, and dragged me back to the cab. The moaning from my assailant triggered a panic attack in me. With the strength of a bull, I managed to finagle my way from Black Tye's grip, and found myself standing directly over top of the masked man. I bent down in front of the coward ass nigga, when Black-Tye pulled off his mask. All I could do was spit in Ray-Ray's face. Alarmed that the sirens seemed to come closer, we hopped back in the cab, and fled the scene.

I looked out the back of the window, because I couldn't believe what had just happened. In a sick way, I felt partially good about what I'd done; the other part of me knew I was going straight to hell.

My mind raced. Why would Ray-Ray do some bullshit like that? I wondered. I knew he was jealous, but I didn't know envy could be deadly. One thing was for sure- Binky would be proud of the way I handled things. *At least I still got the product.*

About an hour went by before Binky met up with us. Although he'd heard about what happened, he waited to meet on purpose. As soon as he walked up to me, he stared. With his hands in his pocket he spoke softly. "Do you understand what happened, Kim?"

I shook my head while managing to keep it lowered.

"Ray- Ray couldn't take the competition. He plotted to take your shit, and then have me handle you. But it got back to me, so I set him up and let it happen."

"I think I killed him," I spoke softly.

"Nah . . . .Tye had already done it. Go home and don't worry. Keep your mouth shut," Binky ordered.

On the way home, the block was hot. Everybody was talking about Ray-Ray getting shot. I thought to myself, *fuck Ray-Ray. He tried to rob me pussy-ass nigga.* All I could think about was only if my mother knew.

All I needed to keep me sane was Binky's voice in my head. "Don't worry," I kept repeating. Hearing that made me feel so much better. Every time I thought about Binky's orders, my smiles would widen.

***

Chapter 6

After school, I took the bus to Latisha's block instead of getting off at my usual stop. I needed to spend a little quality time with Latisha. She told me we hadn't been kickin' it lately, and was feeling like I didn't have time for her anymore. She claimed I was on some ol' brand-new bullshit. I didn't want to set off suspicion from any of my crew, so I needed to at least pretend to be normal.

As soon as I walked in Latisha's house, Binky was the first person I saw. Him just chillin in the house was a strange site. I prayed that he would notice my new low-cut shirt that cost me a big portion of my earnings. My smile spread across my entire face. Hoping that Latisha wouldn't notice, I spoke to Binky casually. He returned the greeting in the same manner. Things were way too quiet, so I broke the dry mood. "I got a message from the girl's by Rhonda's house."

"What girls?" he asked, as if he was irritated.

"The ones who are always in your face." I looked at Latisha to help me tease. She was so into her Jet magazine, she ignored me.

"Tell 'em I'm not interested; tell 'em to try my baby brotha. He's the one who focuses on testin' new pussy." Binky got up off the couch, slipped me a note in between our laughs, and walked away. Even though I was playing catch-up with my good friend, I missed Binky's presence.

Latisha and I had a good time for the next few hours. Although we had totally different interest, I looked up to her. She was real fast. Between her big time twenty-year-old boyfriend and her 36 C cup, she was considered the most experienced of the crew, sexually that is. So I sat and listened, as she talked nasty to every guy that called her house. She even explained in detail to one guy how she liked to be licked like a lollipop. For me, that was straight nasty. What Latisha didn't know was that *sexy shit* meant nothing to me; I'm all about the cash.

"Kim, I'ma hook you up with my new man's brother." Latisha smacked her lips.

"No thanks," I said.

"Girl, they spend that loot. Who do you think paid for this new color in my hair?"

She leaned in closely, so I could get a good look at her hair, but the site of her butt cheeks hanging from her daisy-dukes turned my stomach. I gave Latisha a disapproving look. "I'm not into carrot-colored hair." We laughed together because she knew that she changed her hair color weekly, and I was *never* impressed. Besides, Latisha's hair was already short enough to be rolled with rice.

As soon as I got home, I checked my instructions from Binky. The note said to deliver my package to the man with the freckles, but this time he would be standing on the corner with his pit-bull. Instantly, I called Rhonda's brother begging for a ride. Mr. Prince wouldn't work for this assignment.

After getting a favorable response, I hurried to my bedroom, put my package behind my new boom box, and grabbed my history book. The chapter test was coming soon, and I didn't know shit. School had basically become secondary in my life, but clearly, I had to get right in order to graduate.

As Rhonda's brother Sam pulled up, I grinned knowing that my plan was in order. Staying at their house was becoming a ritual. Surely, my welcome was being worn out. Not really sure about how the rest of her family felt about me, I knew Sam was cool; he never really got in my business. He assumed that I was keeping his sister company.

After we arrived at Rhonda's crib, we stayed outside for about thirty minutes bull-shittin', until I was ready to make my move. We started half way up the street, when

I spotted my man. The freckled-face gentleman was there on the corner, but he was talking to some woman with a long red wig on. I circled the block getting a good look before I let the connect see me. I didn't know whether to deliver the package or not, because I didn't know someone was going to be with him.

I instructed Rhonda to stay put as I walked toward him. I hesitated once I was nearly three feet away. My eyes zoomed in on the woman trying to get a good look. Her face couldn't be seen, but her boots stood out-*tall, fuck-me, multicolored boots on the block.* The expression on my face must have prompted him to ask the lady to leave. Within seconds, she walked off without an additional warning. My first thought was that she was a trick, but after checking out her Donna Karen gear, I was sure that wasn't the case.

I studied her every move as she worked the neighborhood locals with conversation. Once she stopped at the dark blue car near the end of the block, I decided she wasn't a threat, and made my move.

I walked up to the freckled face man, gave him the package without stopping, and walked around the corner. Just as I rounded the corner, I heard men running and shouting. At first, the words were mumbled from the excitement. But then it clicked. "Hands up!"

"Oh shit," I yelled to Rhonda.

"Hit the ground, and put your hands behind your head!" I heard someone scream. I was scared! I thought

they were talking to me, even though I was running faster than a sprinter in the 50-yard dash.

We dashed down the street at top speed. Rhonda in front of me was on the verge of having a heart attack. "Kim, you think they saw you?" she said slowing her pace.

"Who?" I asked, trying to play it cool.

"The fuckin' police. That's who the hell that was! " Rhonda stopped and held her knees in an attempt to catch her breath. "You know, squad cars, lights, and sirens!"

I wanted to play strong in front of Rhonda, but couldn't. As soon as the first tear fell from her eyes, I grabbed her. "It's okay Rhonda. Nobody saw us, and definitely, not you."

My heart was pounding like a drum by the time we reached Rhonda's porch. I snatched the door open so fast; it almost came off the hinges. Out of breath, I asked Sam to give me a ride home. "Now," I said politely. I wanted to get home before my mother.

"W*hat in the hell happened to you?" Sam asked with concern. " I thought you were staying?" He looked at Rhonda before becoming suspicious. "Something happened. You two look like somebody up to no good!"*

"L*et's go," I said, cutting the conversation short. " We got chased by a dog. So we ran like hell to get away from him." I shot Rhonda a look that said* you *better agree.*

Rhonda ignored my look and pulled me to the side. "I

definitely deserve some extra pay for this." She rolled her eyes and left the room.

On the ride home, Sam and I passed by the corner. I noticed the same car that I saw the lady in the red wig talking to, with a siren placed in the window. The doors were wide open and made it easy to notice the freckled face man sitting in handcuffs. I turned my head quickly, as we passed the lady with the wig. My adrenaline pumped! Without delay, I glanced, trying to catch a glimpse of her face. Not much could be made out, but once again her boots stood out; now that's a bad bitch, I thought! *Am I in trouble?* I hope she wasn't gonna come for me next. *Were they trying to catch me too? Or were they just trying to catch the freckled face man?* So many thoughts continued to bounce around in my head.

After I reached home, I calmed my nerves a bit when the chain was securely on the door. I went straight to the phone to make my calls. Thank God my momma wasn't home from work yet. I called Binky and didn't ask for Latisha this time. When he answered I told him to meet me in thirty.

"I'm coming to you," he said.

When I heard the dial tone, I thought, *my place.* Oh, hell no. I know I'm gonna be in some deep shit if somebody sees him here.

But this was important. I paced the floor for the next forty-five minutes waiting for Binky's arrival. I thought about everything, from who knew about the drop, to how much time I'd get in jail.

Suddenly, I heard three light knocks. Opening the door, Binky walked in like we were ready for a board meeting. "Kim, you a'ight," he said, removing the black hoodie from his head.

"Yeah. I just can't believe that shit went down like that."

"You handled it?"

"Ah huh . . . but I was scared as shit. Binky, I think somebody was tryna set all us up."

" Why you say that?" he asked slightly bothered.

"There was this fashionably dressed woman with a red wig on the corner when I got there. She left when I delivered the package, but she was still there later when the police was on the scene." I breathed nervously. "Somethin' ain't right wit' her."

"Can you point her out, if we see her again?"

"I couldn't see her face that good."

"Don't worry. You did good." Binky moved closer and peeled three hundreds from his stack. This was the first time I noticed the thickness of his lips. "Kim, you know I'd kill a mothafucka, before I let you go to jail, right?"

I smiled as I noticed Binky scan my living room. "Damn, how long y'all had that T.V.," he said scoping out the 1980 Zenith.

"Too long. Hey, we can't all live the life of the rich and famous." We laughed lightly until Binky grabbed hold of my chin. "I'm gonna make sure you always a'ight."

At that moment, I was straight hypnotized. He could see that I was catching feelings, and was hesitant about making his move. When his lips met mine, my body got the chills, and my nipples hardened. I never expected Binky to be so gentle. I tried to remember the last boy I'd kissed, and couldn't. But the kiss that Binky was laying on me was sure to never be forgotten. Just as his tongue was about to touch my tonsils, my momma's key was heard in the door.

Binky pushed me slightly disconnecting the two of us. As soon as my momma opened the door, my speech was well thought-out. Binky stood relaxed, while I nervously inched him toward the opened door.

"Oh, Momma, you remember Latisha's brother don't you?"

She examined him from top to bottom like she was searching for a stain on his outfit. "Don't recall," she said sarcastically. Momma stood in front of Binky without moving. With the door still wide open, I stepped around Binky to make the move for him.

"Al right Binky, tell Latisha thanks for sending my stuff," I said, givin' him an escape.

"Nice seeing you again," Ms. Reynolds, Binky said, in the most courteous tone he could muster.

Momma cracked a devious smile as Big Mike came rolling through the door. His oversized frame overshadowed Momma, and gave the impression that trouble had arrived. Binky's calm demeanor changed instantly. Watching the body language between the two had me on edge. Like long lost friends, the embrace they exchanged threw me for a loop.

"I told you we gotta talk," my dad said to Binky. His fingertip pointed so close to Binky's face, I just knew he would react. At first I thought he was talking to me.

"I been waitin' on you playa. Get at me when you can," Binky said as he walked away without giving me, or my dad a second thought.

When the door shut, I sped off in the direction of my room. My father was ruining my life. For once, I'm getting' money, and today- almost got some lovin'.

***

The church parking lot was packed like sardines full of fancy cars, limos and undercover police vehicles. As soon as Big Mike managed to find a park, I started to feel sad again knowing we were headed to pay our respects. While walking toward the front of the church, I spotted Latisha kickin' it with some of the neighborhood thugs. Her skirt was short enough that her butt cheeks could be seen beneath the skirt. I stopped dead in the front, and told Momma, I'd be in shortly. This was my opportunity to show off my new black Donna Karen dress. People weren't used to seeing me dressed this way, so a little extra time on the runway was perfect.

I watched my momma and Big Mike head through the large double doors when a young girl stopped Big Mike. "Hello, Mike," she said in a sassy tone.

Big Mike shot her a nonchalant wave and guided my mother down the aisle. I watched closely as the young girl followed them step by step down the aisle. Her face was familiar, but I couldn't figure out where I knew her from. She was probably someone that I didn't like, 'cause the way she swung her weave like that was her real hair, pissed me off.

Latisha moved close to me to let me know she was going to sit down, but I decided to wait near the front a few more minutes checking out the scenery. All the familiar faces were in attendance; Sam, Rhonda, Mr. Jack's employees and not to mention 5.0. When I spotted the white officer from the incident the other day, I decided to sit down.

I sashayed down the aisle hoping someone would notice my new out-fit and the eye shadow that took me through serious changes to put on perfectly. After spotting my momma near the front, I squeezed directly between her and Big Mike. Surprisingly, to his left, sat the same young mysterious girl who spoke to him when we entered the church. This was my chance to get a real good look. I bit my bottom lip in deep jealously when I saw the big hoop diamond earrings in her ear that read *TEE TEE, along with the matching gold chain.* Before I could scan the rest of her body, the choir stood and the funeral was about to begin. I turned to my left, then my right in search of Binky. He was nowhere to be found. As soon as I eased my head back around, Tee-Tee had made her way into my father's arms. She sat there sniffling, and leaning on him like she knew Mr. Jack real good. *I ain't never seen the winch.* But the last straw was when Mike reached over and consoled her with a hug. What in the fuck was going on?

My first reaction was to hall off and hit the bitch! Was she tryna play my momma? Who the fuck was she? Then, Big Mike reached over and touched momma's shoulder too.

The choir was starting to sound real good, 'cause people got to shoutin' and catching the Holy Ghost. The preacher was puttin' it on us like the Sunday morning service. I started to get another look at Ms. Tee-Tee when Mr. Jack's wife started to breakdown really bad. She ran up to the casket and held on tightly. She screamed, "Why . . . Father. Why?" No one could even hold her together. She cried so hard that I felt bad for her, but in the back of my mind, I thought about what Binky had said, *'She's around Raleigh giving Mr. Jack's money to another man.'* Umh . . . she needed to sit her ass down and be quiet.

My thoughts drifted to my own relatives. For the first time, we were sitting together like a real family. I thought about how my father had missed so much in my life. I thought about how I always wanted to pay him back. But at times like this, you think about forgiveness. I guess I should forgive him, considering I'm his only child. He might need me one day in life, or vice-versa.

I stopped daydreaming, and focused on the preacher's words about Mr. Jack. He spoke about the kind-hearted man that he was, and how he would help everyone out in the community that needed him. The preacher spoke such nice words about Mr. Jack, that I felt a lot better about him passing away. I got scared for a moment, thinking about my grandma's superstitions. My Granny Beck told me that 'death always comes in threes,' but that was some ol' superstitious bullshit .

Before I knew it, the casket was being opened one last time at Donna's request. I sat motionless wanting to remember Mr. Jack alive. Suddenly, Binky and Chanel walked by me and stepped to the front to view the body. They both looked my way, but ignored me as they walked by. What in the hell is this shit? Why is Chanel with Binky? I asked to come with him. What if Chanel is involved with Binky? If she is, why hasn't she told me? I was mad as hell about these two showing up here together. I need to get to the bottom of this. Somebody needs to tell me something! My gut feeling was that something wasn't right.

The funeral was almost over, and the preacher asked everyone to stand and say a prayer. I needed a good prayer because I was doing some wrong shit, and I knew it. As the preacher prayed, I just started to cry all over myself. I don't know what came over me, but it worked my soul real good. My father reached to give me support, but my shoulders stiffened in return.

As the funeral came to a close, we all followed Mr. Jack's casket outside the church doors. The funeral directors scurried around in a chaotic state trying to get the people to their cars. I watched thoroughly as the Toyota Cressida with the New York tags pulled up. The car slowed as if the driver was looking for something, and not they're to pay his respects. I noticed it was the same guy I'd seen talking to Binky before. Strangely, I was feeling the Dread. His long, knotty braids turned me on the most, followed by his sense of mystery. Although I could do away with the red, black, and green toboggan, it was workable. Rough dudes were becoming a must have.

In the midst of my daydreaming gunshots rang out! The target unknown. One of the bullets bounced off the hearse into a car window. I scrunched up my face noticing that my momma hadn't moved. "C'mon, Momma," I yelled. People took off running. Some leaped over car hoods and some hid beneath the vehicles. Instead of running for my life, I was still analyzing shit. I couldn't figure out why anyone would be shooting at Mr. Jack's funeral. I couldn't believe it. I was in total shock.

Between the shattering of glass and hysterical cries, I

couldn't focus. All of a sudden, three more police cars came flying from the top of the hill, and jumped out of their cars with their guns drawn. All I could think about was if anyone had gotten hit, but I couldn't tell from the commotion. My momma grabbed my hand, and I fell losing her grip. As I tried to get up, someone stepped right over me. It was Rhonda. She looked me square in the eye and kept going. I wondered why in the hell she didn't stop to help me. Before I knew it, momma had snatched me up, and we jetted to the car.

. When we were finally safe, I asked my mother, "Where's my father?" She said, "Don't worry, he'll be at the car shortly. I guess he's making sure everyone is okay."

"Everyone like who? We need help!"

As soon as the police secured the scene, and the ambulance arrived, I asked my mother to go see what was wrong. She said, "Your dad will let us know when he gets to the car, Kim."

Waiting on my father to get to the car, drove me crazy. It felt like it was going to be another year before I would see him again. Why was it taking him so long? It did give me time to re-wind the flashbacks of what had happened. I started to get worried, wondering if Binky and Chanel were alright. I didn't see them at all. I sat back impatiently.

After a few minutes, Binky walked right by our car, and didn't even look my way. I panicked because things were clearing out, and I still didn't see my dad. I said a quick prayer. "Dear Lord, keep my father out of harm's way. And forgive me for all my nastiness. I know he might not be the best daddy, but he's all mine."

"Amen," my mother said. She smiled even in the midst of the chaos.

My prayer was answered quickly. My father walked toward the car. I jumped out, met him halfway, and hugged him tightly. He looked at me like I was an imposter. He didn't have to say anything, his expression said it all. That was probably the first hug we exchanged since I was in the 3rd grade.

When he got in the car my momma asked him what had happened. He said, "Somebody shot Mr. Jack's wife."

"Is she dead?" I asked.

"No, the EMS people said she is in bad condition, but they said it looks like she's going to make it."

Wanting answers, I asked my dad did anyone see who did it. Without answering, he turned to give me a suspect look. I'm sure he wondered about my interest.

When we got home, our phone was ringing like crazy. Everybody was calling my moms talking about it. They couldn't believe what had happened. The supposed-to-be-story was that Donna was fooling around with drugs and that she had stolen some guy's money. Everyone in our house knew Faye, would be calling back before dark. I was praying this time that

Faye's shit would be halfway right or even close to the truth.

My father was in the background putting his two cents in as my mother talked. After only thirty minutes, I had reverted back to the same angry Kim. Hell, he's only been in town a few days, and already packed to leave. I shoulda' bet money on this nigga's length of stay. I glanced at him wondering when he would be back. He claimed that he was going back to D.C. for a while to clear some things up *Ump . . . I'll believe that when hell freezes over.*

I wanted to tell my dad so badly to shut the hell up when he talked about the shooting, but I couldn't disrespect him. But the last straw was when he came out the mouth sour to me. "Kim, now remember what I said about Binky. Leave him and the streets alone." If he says another word, his ass was about to get it. I thought to myself, *I miss you daddy but take your ass home. If you were andling' your business, I wouldn't have to do this.* I always had an excuse about me doing the wrong things.

***

Chapter 7

"Ms. Willis, is Chanel home?" I asked.

"No baby," she answered while opening the door slightly.

"Do you know where she is?"

Ms. Willis chuckled,"Y'all can't do without each other huh?"

I gave up a counterfeit smile. What she didn't know was that I wasn't here for pleasure, it was business.

"Did Chanel tell you we're moving to Durham?" she continued in her deep southern voice.

"Noooooo . . . . When is that?" I asked, shocked.

Mrs. Willis squeezed my hand tightly. "Not right now, but Chanel will fill you in."Her facial expression saddened a bit. "I think she went up to the next circle to meet Latisha. They on some cheerleading team," she said, like she really believed a team had been formed in Southgate.

I almost choked on my own spit. I couldn't believe what Ms. Willis had just said. She had no idea what Chanel was getting herself into. But, I intended to get to the bottom of it. It really surprised me to know that Chanel would get involved with Binky. She was the one in our crew who didn't normally fool with niggas. Her dreams of going to college and getting out of the hood had me even believing that shit.

"Kim, you okay?" Ms. Willis asked diverting me from my daze.

"Yes, I'm fine. Tell Chanel to call me when she gets in?"

"Sure will baby, and how's your mother?"

"She's fine. I'll tell her you asked about her."

I hurried to the next circle in search of the two traitors. Chanel was easy to spot. She was the only girl in our hood who stood as tall as the fellas. Her long, wavy hair, hung below her baseball cap. As usual, Binky stood like a soldier guarding his fort. Pissed at them both, I couldn't get up the hill fast enough.

As I approached the steps where everyone sat, I saw Chanel with a sweater jacket on just like mine. I couldn't believe it. My defiant stare focused on Chanel first by the time I turned to Binky, it was pure disgust. "What's up Chanel?"

She shrugged her shoulders, and took two steps back

from me like I had HIV. "I've gotta make a run," she said.

"Chanel, we gotta talk when you get back," I said talking to her backside.

"No problem," Chanel said as she pushed the sleeves up on her jacket like she was about to put in work.

I leaned back on the railing watching my girl head down the block. Since Binky and I were alone, I figured we'd get a chance to talk. "Is Chanel doing a great job like me? I see she's the captain of the team."

Binky started to laugh. "Take care of your end, and I'ma worry 'bout the rest."

I really wanted to hear what he was gonna say about Chanel and me. Everything started to run through my mind. One thing for sure is that I couldn't wait to tell Chanel my whole story, because I knew she was gonna tell me hers. I told Binky bye, and that I'd holla at him tomorrow. He stood up and kissed me on my cheek. "So, you not workin' today?" he asked, removing the straw from his mouth.

"When was the last time you kissed Chanel's cheek?" At this point I was behaving like an elementary school student. I knew Binky had feelings for me, but figured he didn't have time to pursue me.

"Grow up, Kim. I need you to handle some more business."

"When?" I asked, as if I was doing him a favor.

"Now," he said. "I'ma have my people pick you up, in

twenty minutes."

"Where?"

"In front of Mr. Jack's store. Binky knelt down and removed a small brown bag from his unlaced Timberland boot. I jerked backward when he raised up and pulled me close. Just when I thought he was gonna make a move I licked my lips. The next thing I knew, Binky had slipped the package in my jacket, and let me go.

"Don't keep playin' wit' me, Binky."

He ignored me. "My folks will take you to Church's Chicken on New Bern Avenue to meet Johnny Dollar again. This time, he'll be in a blue Jeep Cherokee. Ya follow me?"

"Yea . . . Yea . . . Yea . . ." I nodded my head in agreement.

"Keep your cheerleader jacket on, and walk up to the car. Don't speak, turn around and go inside Church's."

By now, my eyes had rolled back inside my head. I folded my arms and tapped my feet. When Binky's slinky hand backslapped me like a mack truck, I completely freaked out. I held my face and looked away from him for a second. "Fuck you," I shouted.

"I like that," he boasted! "That means you gettin' some heart!" He grinned. "Now, are you ready to be serious, or should I give one of your girls ya job?" Binky wore a harsh look on his face, that gave no leniency to my tears.

This nigga always talking ‘bout loyalty. *Hell, he has none,* I thought. “Binky, I need this money.”

“Then, go get it!” When Johnny follows you in the restaurant, he’ll go into the men’s bathroom. Order a twenty-piece mix with extra dressing from the Flava Flav look-a-like. Order only from him. Take the chicken box to Johnny in the bathroom, and get back in your ride. The driver will bring you back to the block. Don’t call me until tomorrow around 4 o’clock.

“Got it.” I walked off with a swagger. Binky didn’t realize that he was creating a monster. I checked my watch, and headed for my pick up spot. Right on time, my ride was there. I hopped in headed for Church’s.

No sooner than I arrived, the blue Cherokee was parked in perfect position. I followed Binky’s orders to a tee. With an arrogant smirk on my face I walked close enough to the Cherokee to be seen by Dollar. He acknowledged me silently, as I kept walking into the restaurant, and waited in line. The Flava Flava look-a-like had no idea who I was until I got to the register.

“I’d like twenty-two mixed pieces with extra dressing.”

“No doubt. The worker quickly opened a door behind the register and appeared with an already boxed Church’s bag. Sweat formed upon his forehead as if he’d ran a marathon. His eyes were crossed like a crazed maniac, as he handed me the bag.

“Thanks,” I said, grabbing hold tightly.

I rushed slightly around the corner to the men's bathroom. I stood there momentarily wondering whether or not to knock, when Dollar opened the door. I threw him the bag, no dialogue whatsoever, and jetted.

As soon as I hit the corner, I panicked. Three officers had their badges pulled out and asking the guy behind the register to step from behind the counter. My eyes grew to the size of Tupac's ego. I stared them down, wondering if they wanted me too.

Before I knew it, the guy behind the counter sprinted two yards from the register, and jumped through the drive thru window! Gunshots popped off. At first, I bobbed and weaved perfectly until one of the officers fired back in my direction. Crouched down beside the trashcan, I watched the heavy-set officer take off running after Flava Flav. In the next instant, Johnny Dollar was being cuffed.

As everyone in the restaurant began to feel safe again, I made my move to leave unnoticed, amongst the confusion. I was already shaking in my boots, but when Johnny's eyes met mine, it worsened. Scared shitless, I ran out of the restaurant like a criminal in a citywide foot chase. Reaching the outside, I turned to look for my ride. Other than, the Raleigh P.D. cruisers, the parking lot was damn near empty. I paused trying to decide where to go. I needed a place to lay low for a couple of hours until I could see if the police were on to me.

With no time to think clearly, I took off running.

After blocks and blocks, I felt like giving up. With my adrenaline pumping, and heart beating rhythmically, an hour later I ended up on my block.

As I approached Chanel's house, she and Mrs. Willis could be seen walking into the house. I yelled out to Chanel, gasping for air. Before they made it in the doorway, Chanel turned my way. Although my hand placed over my rapidly beating heart didn't calm my breathing, it did raise her suspicion. When Chanel looked back and saw my jacket, and the fear in my eyes, her jaw dropped. Instantly, she walked backwards telling her mom, she'd be out front with me. I wanted to be mad at Chanel for playin' me earlier, but I needed her.

We hugged one another, because we both needed strength. The game that we thought was protected by Binky had now become dangerous. It was obvious the teenage stuff was over; we were in with the big boyz. Chanel and I were on the same page and didn't even know it. We sat down on her steps filling each other in from the day we got our jackets. I asked Chanel how long she had been dealing with Binky and she said for about three months. She asked me the same thing, and I told her two months. I told Chanel that I enjoyed working for Binky, and that I liked him a lot. All Chanel did was laugh like she always did. She said that her job was to collect the money, so I guess that left me to drop off the packages. Chanel asked me if I had ever seen the guys that Binky always talked to in the Cressida with the

New York plates.

I said, "Yes, what about it?" She said that she didn't trust them around Binky, but she wasn't going to say anything. I didn't tell Chanel that me and Dread already made eye contact the last few times that I saw him. Talking about Dread sent our conversation on Donna Jack. Chanel said that she heard Binky talking to the Jamaican with New York plates; I told her that I had already named him 'Dreads'. She said that Donna owed him money for some cocaine. I couldn't figure out how Donna knew the Dread from New York. I needed to find out more about this lady.

In the middle of our conversation, Chanel stood and gave me a hug. "I'm sick, Kim."

"What are you talkin' about?"

"I've got Lupus." Chanel spoke sadly.

"Chanel, stop right there." I held my hand in front of her face. "What is that?"

"It's an illness that takes over your blood cells."

"You're not dying are you?" I asked teary eyed. I didn't know whether to be strong for my girl, or break down and cry.

"With the right treatments, I'll be fine," Chanel answered. The bad part about it is that it keeps you in the hospital all the time." She hesitated and looked as if she was scared to tell me the rest.

"What is it?" I asked, afraid to hear the rest.

"We're moving to Durham, so I can be near Duke

Hospital. I'll be going there often to take tests, and learn more about how to deal with the disease." She smiled slightly. "Plus, my mother is finally going to get the job of her dreams, or at least the job she's been wanting."

I was so heartbroken, that I could not respond. I turned my head, away from Chanel momentarily. I had to be strong.

"Kim," she said, touching my shoulder. "You don't plan on doing this for long do you?"

"Of course not," I said, trying to pacify my sick friend.

"We're going to college next year, remember." She wanted me to agree, and I did for her sake. But we weren't on the same page. I was determined to get paid. My talk game was as good as a seasoned dealer and getting better by the day. Yes, I had run into some situations that scared me shit-less, but it has made me tough.

When Chanel and I finally finished our conversation, I had her call my house to make sure the coast was clear. When she called pretending to look for me, my momma sounded normal, saying she was expecting me soon.

That night, I lay in bed thinking about the past few months of my life. I couldn't believe I'd gone from rags to ghetto-riches; from fatherless to having Big Mike back in my life; then, from hanging with my girls, to pushing weight. And I certainly didn't expect to be hounded by the police. I had gotten myself into some serious mess.

There seemed to be a way out, but not one I'd take. For now, my plan was to lay low, and warn Binky. We have an empire to build. Like Binky says, *everyone is disposable.*

***

Chapter 8

The alarm clock sounded at 6:45 a.m. sharp. I knew I wasn't going to school, but Momma opened my door and turned on the lights like everything was normal.

I got up, and stumbled around my room with my eyes half closed. "What's wrong with you?" Momma asked.

"I'm sick," I answered groggily. My hair stood straight up on top of my head, 'cause I purposely didn't roll it the night before. As soon as Momma walked toward her room, I opened the toilet seat, and made a loud gagging sound. My coughs were exaggerated even more, as I tried to bring attention to my fake sickness. It wasn't long before Momma rushed to the doorway.

"Girl, what's wrong with you?"

I sluggishly wiped my mouth with the ball of toilet

paper, held firmly in my hand. Quickly, I flushed the toilet, and closed the commode.

"*I am so sick," I said, turning to my mother. "I can't go to school today.*"

"Do you need to go to the doctor?"

"Nah. I think it's something I ate last night." I walked back toward my room. "I'll be okay once it all comes out."

Momma didn't want to leave me, but I convinced her that I would be alright; if I wasn't doing better later, then she could take me to the doctor. She agreed, and said that she would call me on her first break at 10:00. The phone rang in the midst of our conversation. Ms. Faye, herself, was back on the hotline. When I answered, I could hear Ms. Faye talking to someone in her house. She was saying, "*Girl, you don't know a damn thing about cooking chittlings. You done sat there and half cleaned them, and want somebody to eat'um when you finish. Hell, I ain't eatin' them damn things like that!*"

I said, "H*ello, hello.*"

"*Lord child, I didn't hear you pick up the phone, this damn sista of mine, done half-cleaned these chittlings. Is your momma home?*"

"Yeah. Here she is," I said, handing her the phone.

Damn, Ms. Faye must've gone for my momma's guts. Seconds into the conversation, she had signs of disappointment on her face. What could Faye have told her on the phone? She talked to Faye a few more minutes, then hung up.

"Is everything okay?" I asked.

"Sure, baby. Faye was just telling me some new information."

"So why are you looking like that?"

"Like what, Kim?" she said changing her demeanor. She gave me a half-ass smile. "I'm okay."

It didn't 'fly with me, but I let it go for now, since I'm supposed to be sick. I knew she had gotten some bad news, but she just wouldn't tell me. As soon as she left for work, I jumped straight up and called Binky.

In no time, he answered. Immediately, I started to fill him in on the night before. I held the phone in shock, when the dial tone sounded in my ear. "No, this mothafucka didn't hang up on me," I said in anger. I slammed the phone down, took two seconds to think, and dialed his ass again.

He picked up on the first ring. "I'll see you when you get outta school," he said in an irritated tone.

"I'm not going to school today," I yelled!

"Then, I'm coming over." He hung up.

"Oh shit," I mumbled. I jumped off the bed, and ran to fix my hair. I wasn't quite sure how long he would take, but looking a mess was not an option. I gave myself what Ms. Faye would call a 'ho bath', trying to freshen up for Binky. Ten minutes had gone by, and I was just slipping my Guess jeans on, when the phone rang. I jetted to the phone thinking Binky had changed the plan.

"Hello," I answered energized.

"Well, you sound better already," my momma said.

Instantly, I changed my pitch. "I'm trying to get motivated while I'm studying."

"Thank you Jesus," she said. "At least you're well enough to get some work done. You know Kim, graduation is around the corner."

"I know Momma. I'ma get my grades up. Let me try to read a little," I said, hearing light knocks at the door. "I'm still a little queasy."

"Okay. I'll be home by five."

"See ya."

I ran to the door forgetting that I still had my pajama shirt on.

"What's up?" Binky said, entering the apartment. Instantly, his eyes focused on my boobs, which hung outside my pink-laced pajama top. Noticing his stare, I used my left hand to cover up.

"You don't got shit that I ain't seen."

I laughed, and just fixed my top as best I could.

"So Kim, why you still insist on talking over the phone?" he asked. "Don't you know 5.0 might be listening?"

"They don't need to listen, cause' they see us everywhere we go!"

"So you still think it's cool to talk on the phone."

I shrugged my shoulders. "But . . ."

"But nothin'. Talkin' on tape might cost your young

ass, twenty-five to life. Now I know you probably wanna talk about what went down at Church's, but you gotta learn; there's a time and place for everythang."

"You don't understand." I talked a mile a minute. "The police was there, Dollar got locked up, gun shots were fired, and the guy behind the register jumped through the fuckin' drive through window!" Out of breath, I ended with, "I think 5.0 knew I was in on it!"

Binky pulled me close. He looked into my eyes and said, "Kim, everything you do wrong comes with a price. This game will forever get you rich and will always let you down. So, if you continue to run with me, be ready to handle anything, at any time."

I stood with glassy eyes. This was becoming more than I could handle. I had thuggish tendencies, but damn. Binky spoke as if this was what I should expect. I looked at him wide-eyed. "What if Johnny Dollar tells the police that I was the one who gave him the package?"

"He won't, but this game is full of snitches. Be careful, and never let anyone put you in position to be told on. I fuck with real niggas. We go hard until the end. Actually Kim, I'd rather do life then to snitch on my folks."

"Damn, I thought. Is that what this shit is all about. *I ain't going to jail for no mothafuckin' body.*

Binky said, "It's hard to get out of the game, Kim."

I nodded like I was finally understanding. "Then let's get this shit started. I want more action, and more responsibilities, but I know it comes with more changes." *And hopefully more money.*

"I think you're ready. Have you talked to your father lately?"

"Why you ask?"

Binky began to twitch. I knew something was on his mind. "I heard your dad was coming back to the area for good."

"How would you know that?"

"I've got my ways."

"He didn't tell us nothin like that." I thought about telling Binky what my daddy said about him, but I changed my mind. "You seem to know, more about his comings and his goings than I do."

Binky laughed at me. "You think you're so smart, don't you?"

"You know it nigga!"

"You still wet behind the ears, and don't even know it."

"You think so," I said, closing in on Binky's lanky frame.

He was definitely reading my mind, because without speaking, his hand was already two-thirds of the way up my shirt. I pulled him even tighter, as his dick grew with excitement. Binky gripped my face with his rough hands, and backed me up to the couch. He kissed me with force, like he was dying from hunger, and I was his next meal.

In between the wet slurps, I managed to say, "Uh . . .

uh, maybe we better stop, Binky."

"Why?" he asked, catching a breath.

"'Cause I can't have no babies."

"I got somethin' for that."

Like a magician, Binky pulled a condom from his back pocket. Damn, I thought, *is he always ready like this?* 'Cause surely I'm not trying to be his freak of the week. I don't know how it happened so fast, but the next thing I knew, we were butt naked on my momma's plastic. I held my fist tightly, as Binky tried to stick it in. I thought gritting my teeth would help lessen the pain, but it hurt like hell.

I pretended to be all in it. But when the head made it in, I knew I'd need medical attention. I wanted to scream, but decided against it. I thought about all the nasty things I'd heard from Rhonda and Latisha, but couldn't bring myself to act freaky. At that moment, I wondered if their exotic sex stories were even true, 'cause this shit hurt like hell!

Binky continued to pound like he was in a zone. I squirmed from under his pelvis, to see if he was pleased. Although his face remained buried into the couch, his moans verified his enjoyment. Fortunately, after a few minutes of opening me up, Binky's long yard was starting to bring me some comfort. With a few shift of the hips, I stroked back like a pro.

My sudden movements must've sent Binky into shock. He licked my tits like he was trying to reach the center of a tootsie roll. Second by second, his thrust increased. "Oh shit," he yelled. My pussy tightened as he jerked!

Binky continued to pant, rising off of me. With my head lowered, I made sure not to look at him. My first thought was to run to the bathroom, but didn't know if I could walk. The tingling sensation between my legs had gotten the best of me.

Luckily, Binky made the first move. He lifted my chin. "Kim, you a'ight," he asked.

I nodded.

"Now don't go actin' different on me."

"Whatcha mean?"

"We still gotta be able to work." He smiled. "I'ma grab you a towel."

As soon as Binky walked toward the bathroom, I sighed. Sinking down in the couch, I reflected on what I had done. *Was that considered, good dick*? Before I knew it, Binky and I had done a no no. We were lying chest to chest in my bed. For some reason, Binky came up with the crazy idea to spend the afternoon together. He explained that this was no way near a commitment, but a good opportunity to lay up with someone who wouldn't rob him blind. On one hand, I was proud to know that he trusted me. But on the other, he had told me in so many words, that we were fuckin' for fun. Ain't this some shit! My first time out the gate, and I can't even be on girlfriend status for a day!

After countless hours of talking, Binky realized that three o'clock was approaching. He jumped up saying that he had to meet Chanel for a run. Instantly, I got jealous. "I'm going too." I rolled my eyes and stretched my neck like Chanel was a threat.

"You better stay in," Binky said. "What you gon' say when somebody tells your mother you was out and about?"

I thought about it for a moment and got dressed. "I'll make it back by five o'clock," I said, brushing my hair in place. "Let's go." I threw on a cute UNC baseball cap, followed Binky, like groupies on athletes.

We headed out the door and met Chanel on the corner as planned. When me and Binky walked up together, she looked shocked that I was there. I hugged her to let her know, I didn't want her job. It eased the tension, as Chanel prepared for her run.

Within minutes, we were on Capital Boulevard and pulled in the lot of *Whites Luxury Cars.* Chanel hopped out without instruction, and walked right up to the door. My eyes got big when I noticed her finger motioning for me to come. I turned to Binky for approval. After no response, I pulled my hat down over my eyes, and hopped out to see what Chanel needed. As soon as I was close enough, she pulled me by the arm. Together, we walked inside like two customers in search of a brand new car. The first salesperson was a chubby guy, sporting a plaid overcoat. His first instinct was to run up on us, in search of a sale. Once we were face-to-face, he stared us down as if to say, '*You are too young.*' Chanel's expression told me that she was nervous. I stepped in, "We're looking for . . . What's his name?" I asked Chanel. She stood like a zombie.

"Mr. White?" she stuttered.

The salesperson walked away just as a tall good-looking, white man came out. For a man in his early forties, Mr. White behaved like a young energetic gentleman. Clapping his hands in a cheerful manner, he asked us to follow him to his office. By the time we walked down the narrow, dark hallway, Chanel had pretty much shut down completely. The man made small talk, but I didn't budge. He was way too animated for me. It only took a few minutes for me to grab the duffel bag, and walk out the back door. Chanel trailed behind sweating, like she had no idea what was going on.

When Binky saw me leading the way with the bag in hand, he gave up a strange smirk. As I got closer to him, he pulled slightly away from us, and pointed in the direction of a white 300 CE Benz. I stood there puzzled, until Chanel snapped from her daze. "The keys are in the bag," she finally whispered. "Put the coke on the passenger side under the seat."

I shot my girl a nasty look 'cause she had put me in a bad situation. She knew exactly what to do, but couldn't follow through. Obviously Binky had given her the specific instructions. But, at that point, I knew I'd have to use my own judgment. On the way toward the white Benz, I checked my surroundings for undercover vans, cameras, or surveillance teams. I knew Raleigh P.D. could be near. In the midst of my search, I noticed Chanel searching too. Even though she wasn't worth shit as a hustler, she was still my girl.

I was surprised when the doors unlocked instantly to the Benz. I had imagined I'd have to fumble with the keys for a while, but things were moving smoothly, until the duffel bag wouldn't fit behind the passenger seat. Instantly, I decided the bag would be put in the trunk. Chanel panicked as I made my move. "Binky said put it in the backseat," she rambled.

"It won't fit," I snapped.

"Put it all the way in the back; it'll fit."

"It won't! And instead of fighting with a bag full of drugs in broad daylight, it's going in the trunk!" I slammed the trunk lightly.

Chanel snatched the keys and ran toward the door where Mr. White was talking with a customer. "Excuse me sir, but I believe these are your keys."

Mr. White grabbed the keys politely, "Thank you young lady?"

We safely pulled out of the parking lot shortly after the bag was secure. The clock on Binky's dashboard caused me to panic. "Four fifty two," I yelled. "My momma is gonna kill me! I'll never make it home on time."

***

Chapter 9

I didn't say a word. Innocent until proven guilty went through my mind. I had watched all those T.V. shows; New York Undercover and NYPD Blue. As long as I kept my mouth shut, I would be okay. It was bad enough that my mother got home before me, watched me hop out of Binky's car, and allowed Starsky and Hutch to invade our home. But now, I'm sitting here being chastised by the police, my mother, and her friend. *What fuckin' luck.*

I almost cringed when Ms. Faye began to pace the floor with her arms folded. It was obvious that my mother asked her to come for support, but Ms. Faye had no credibility with the police, or reason to be acting like my parent. Besides, she had her own misfortunes to tend to.

I sat straight faced and glanced out the window as the burly Italian officer talked. Nervously my mother stared into his mouth digesting every word. "So you wanna be a gangsta, huh?" the officer joked.

Disapproving of his ignorance, I scratched my head.

"Do you know where Carlton Lyles works?"

"Who is Carlton Lyles?" I asked sarcastically.

"You really are gullible," the shorter officer interjected. Until now he had been relatively silent as he took notes at the table. His pale-ass was doing alright until he opened his mouth. "We're talking about Binky." He shook his head in disgust.

I got defensive real quick. "How would I know where Binky works? He's my friend's brother. That's it! I'm not his keeper," I ended, after sucking my teeth.

"Oh, that's good." The Italian officer clapped loudly. "I see you've rehearsed."

I rolled my eyes.

"Kim, stop this silly behavior, and talk to officer . . . What's your name again?" my mother said.

"Rodriquez. Officer Rodriquez." While he gave my mother the utmost respect, he was clearly out to get me.

"Kim, your mother is an honorable woman. Let's not play games, and have us search her house. Everybody might have to go downtown?"

Ms. Faye and I just looked at each other. Without delay, I scrolled my brain trying to remember a lesson from Binky on how to handle police searches.

"Go ahead," I snapped. Surely the local news station might wanna know about you questioning a seven-teen year old in her home without a lawyer."

A grin seeped from Ms. Faye's lips. I could tell she was impressed. My mother was already somewhere in between going into cardiac arrest and death. "Listen, young lady. Binky has sold more cocaine in this city than Dennis Rodman has tattoos. He's now wanted for questioning, for the murder of one of his workers, Ray-Ray."

I froze.

"Eye-witnesses say Binky was there at the time of the murder. When was the last time you saw Ray- Ray?"

Ms. Faye finally butted in. "What makes you think she knows anything about Ray Ray?" Like a bodyguard, she moved closer to my side. "In case you didn't notice, she's a damn minor. She don't know nothing 'bout Ray Ray or Binky, so leave her alone."

Rodriquez gave Ms. Faye a disapproving look. She stood boldly with her hands on her hips. "This is going too far. Now if you wanna arrest somebody, arrest me!"

By now my mother was in agreement with Faye. "Maybe the two of you should leave until we can get a lawyer," she saidas she headed to open the door.

Old pale ass spoke. "That's not necessary," he said. "It's Binky we want. If Kim tells us what we need to know, there won't be any trouble. He's the one being investigated. Kim just got herself hooked up with the wrong guy."

My mother's expression showed that she meant business. "Good afternoon gentleman."

"Yes, Mam, I guess we'll be leaving. You know, Kim, prisons are full of young women who protect their boyfriends. And the grave yards are full of young girls who wore cheerleading jackets," Rodriquez said, as he left out of the door.

"He's not my boyfriend," I yelled as the door closed behind them.

Ms. Faye's mouth revved. Her words came out going fifty miles per hour. "Now, Leslie, you know your baby is gettin' beside her damn self. She think don't nobody know." Ms. Faye stood with her hands on her hips. "I got one damn question. How in the hell you gon' be involved wit' somebody and don't know they real name?"

"I'm not involved with Binky! Besides, I know his name; I just ain't no snitch!"

"Yeah . . . . Yeah . . . Yeah. Tell that bull shit to somebody who's gonna believe it." Ms. Faye pretended to play her instrument to mock my excuses. "I suggest you take some dope dealer classes," She laughed hysterically, "'cause you are the poorest hustler I've ever seen."

By now, Momma had lost it. She held the Bible in her hand like she was ready for a sermon. "Faye, I think we need some time."

"Time. Hell, you need more than time. Yo ass need

prayer! And you might need bail money soon, fuckin' around wit' Kim," she said, slamming the door.

On one hand, I was glad Ms. Faye had gone out the door. But a part of me, wanted her to stay, 'cause now I had to face my momma.

"Kim, I've always tried to raise you right," she said sincerely. "I've done my best with what I've had to work with. But child, you gotta use some common sense." She turned the pages of the good book and paused momentarily. "You think you gon' get away with whatever you doing?"

"Momma, I'm not doin' nothing!" My stomach boiled at the thought of lying to the only person who loves me unconditionally. "I hate my life!" I screamed several more times to give myself an excuse to run to my room.

Momma yelled out. "I'll be taking you to school this week," she said.

I was mad as hell.

***

The next morning, my life seemed to move in slow motion. I had been up most of the night thinking about Binky's connection with the young girl who got shot, and how I would warn him about the police. We were supposed to meet after school today, but nothing was going as planned. Since Momma laid down the law, and sentenced me to lockdown, I wasn't sure how I'd get to Binky.

Sluggishly, I moved around my room like a zombie. Almost two hours had passed when my mother finally yelled out, "Let's go!"

My mother stood at the front door like a kernel in the army, ready to move out his soldiers. I headed to the door with my cheerleading jacket in hand, and m y books that I hadn't touched in days. "Oh, forget about this," she said, as she snatched the jacket from my grip.

"Momma, that's not mine!"

"Well, I'll give it back to Latisha." She smirked. "You no longer have any affiliation with this jacket. Do you understand me?" she shouted.

Momma had more street sense than I thought. I wasn't into disrespecting her, so I headed out the door without my jacket.

"Alright," I said, shrugging my shoulders.

It was a beautiful morning, and the front of the school was packed as we pulled up in front of Enloe. Embarrassed, I reached to give Momma an apologetic kiss. Before I could get out of the car good, Chanel, Latisha,, and our wanna be friend Zandy walked up like there was an emergency. "We been waiting on you," Zandy said with reservation.

Zandy was the type of person who was a follower, so I didn't take her seriously. She just wanted to be down with the *in crowd*, so she'd say and do anything to make that happen. The fact that she and Black Tye had been fuckin' lately, turned my stomach.

My mother watched us talk for a few seconds. She looked at me funny as she pulled off. "See you at three," she yelled.

I looked around contemplating on skipping school; but after seeing Mr. Branch, our burly security officer, my plans changed. *Damn*, I thought. *I gotta get up with Binky.*

"Bitch, do you hear me?" Latisha asked, moving within two inches of my face. "Some girl is going round saying she's your sista!"

"What girl? What she look like?" I questioned.

As usual Latisha smacked her lips between every word. "You know that bitch from Longview. They think they better over there."

"Who she be with?" I asked

"She's always by herself." Latisha rolled her neck back and forth as if she had a personal vendetta against this girl. "Oh, you seen her lonely ass before. I would straighten a bitch going round saying she some kin to me."

The late bell rang snapping us all from our huddle. We all headed in different directions toward our classes; except for Latisha and I who had Ms.Porter for first period English. When we walked in, class had already begun. Before I could even sit down good, Ms. Porter's white, oversized ass asked me to give my interpretation of a poem that she knew I hadn't read.

Everyone knew she was being funny, so they took the liberty to laugh. Latisha gave me a look that said, *Fuck that Bitch*, so we joined in, and laughed too. When Ms. Porter realized her weak sarcasm wasn't gonna work, she diverted to teaching again.

"Now, hopefully everyone is almost done with their final analysis of *To Kill a Mocking Bird*." Her eyes zoomed in on me. "If not, keep in mind, my grades are due in two weeks. You will not graduate without passing English."

I opened my English book, trying hard to ignore Ms. Porter for the next fifty minutes. I didn't know why we had to stay in her class so long anyway. English was important, but math was gonna get me paid in life. Latisha was obviously bored to death, 'cause she sat there doodling '*Latisha Gets Around*' all over her composition book. I chuckled after seeing about ten male names listed under each of the three gigantic hearts. *She was definitely becoming a freak, but I ain't mad at her.*

Suddenly Latisha ripped a piece of paper from her tablet, scribbled a few words quickly, and passed it to me. My eyebrows creased when I read the note.

I almost forgot. Binky said meet him tonight at midnight outside of Mr. Jack's store.– Important- He said your mother got you on lock-down.

As soon as I finished reading the note, the bell rang. I wanted to ask Latisha what else Binky said, when Ms.

Porter asked to see me. While the other students exited the room, I stood in front of her desk with my arms folded.

"Kim, do you plan on walking across that stage in three weeks?" Ms. Porter asked.

"Yes, I do," I responded, with too much spunk.

"Well, I suggest you use these last few assignments to pull your grades up. You have a sixty-two average, which means you're in danger of failing."

I tried to pretend like I didn't care. But I knew I had to graduate, and make my momma proud. "I'll get my work in," I said. "I will graduate."

Noticing that my girls Latisha and Chanel, were waiting outside the door, I smiled at Ms. Porter like I'd turned a new leaf. Once in the hallway, the crew bombarded me with questions about my conversation with the teacher.

I didn't answer any of them. As we headed toward the cafeteria. Zandy met us at the entrance and told me that the girl claiming to be my sista, was in the café showing everybody a picture of her and my father.

"How do you know it's my father. You never even seen him," I said to Zandy in a harsh tone. I lunged at her real quick, pretending to want to want to hit her.

Zandy jerked back. "Yeah, but . . . I think she's for real," she stuttered.

I always got a kick out of intimidating Zandy. "Where is she?" I asked, bursting through the double doors. Just then, I thought I'd have an anxiety attack. The necklace that read Tee-Tee stared me in the face. "That's the bitch from the funeral, who sat next to my dad." My eyes nearly popped out of my head.

Tee-Tee walked directly in my path. "Hello," she said walking pass me. Instantly, I fixed my eyes on her outfit. Her clothes were a little too preppy for my taste, but nonetheless, they were pricey. The white pleated skirt, the green and red vest, were all Gucci products. *Where did she get that kinda money*? I wondered.

By now, I had turned and followed Tee-Tee from behind. Her hair hung evenly, way below her shoulders, and bounced as she walked. I followed her for at least thirty more seconds before she stopped and turned to face me.

"What's this about you being my sister," I asked.

"It is what it is?" She hunched her shoulders. "Big Mike didn't tell you?"

We did kinda favor around the eyes. Although I looked more like my dad, she did have his high cheekbones. I was starting to drive myself crazy. "Look Tee-Tee, it all sounds good, but I ain't got no sistas."

"Look at the picture," she said, holding a 4x6 in my direction.

I made a point not to look at the photo. "A picture don't mean shit," I snapped. "Let's make this the end of our fake family reunion." I walked away hoping that Tee-Tee knew I didn't wanna hear no more.

By the end of the day, my head was in need of three Tylenol's with codeine. Between thinking about Tee-Tee and Binky, my nerves had been beat up. When Momma pulled up to the curb, I was actually glad to get in. I turned to my mother considering asking her if she'd ever heard about Tee-Tee, or about Big Mike having any other children. But when momma started her speech about finding a wad of money stashed in my room, I reared back in the seat, and closed my eyes tightly.

***

Chapter 10

Dressed in all black, I blended right into the darkness. Moving swiftly, I looked over my shoulder to make sure Momma hadn't heard me leave out. I was already in the hot seat after she found my money. But if she found out I was leaving the house at midnight, I'm sure eviction would be next. Between the cops, Binky, and the money; she had been watching me like a hawk.

Walking in front of the store, a sense of uneasiness ran through my spirit. I loved Binky like a brother, and a lover, but knowing that the young girl had died wearing the same jacket Binky had me wear, was a bit suspect. Besides, the way he sat with his hands folded on the hood of the car, had me questioning his reason for meeting me so late.

When Binky saw me approaching, he raised off his

Caddy. I couldn't see his face, but he stood straight up like he was ready for battle. Startled, I moved slower and slower. As I got closer, the reflection of the street lights, revealed a .357 by his side. Shocked, I took two steps back. Suddenly, Binky rushed me like a defense player rushing a quarterback. I tried to scream, but the pressure from his hand, over my mouth, had me on hush.

"Kim, whassup wit' you?" he whispered. "Why you bringing attention to us?"

He hugged me gently as he removed his hand from my face. Out of breath, I gasped for air. "I . . . I . . . I saw the . . . gun."

"The gun is for my protection. I'on know who watching me, or who to trust." He cupped my chin. "One's things for sure. I trust you."

I took a deep breath. Nothing could be more perfect. Directly under the Mr. Jacks' store sign, he kissed me deep and hard, like he wanted to fuck. Or at least like I had a chance at being his girl.

"Let's take a ride," he said, guiding me to the car. Binky saw me look back at the store and decided it was a good time to share the news. "Did you hear that Mr. Jacks's store was up for sell?" Binky opened the door for me like a perfect gentleman.

"What? When did that happen?"

He answered me once inside the car. "I just found out about it a couple of days ago," he said, pulling from the curb. "Donna need money bad."

"Ain't she still in the hospital."

"She's out, but she still gotta eat."

For Binky the store didn't mean much, but I started wishing, I could buy that store for my mother. She could quit working for the pennies that never covered the bills anyway.

Binky saw me in a daze. "What'cha thinkin' 'bout?" he asked.

"Everything." I watched him intently.

Quickly, his fingers ran across my thighs, and landed directly between my legs. It felt good, but I needed answers. Even though, I didn't stop him, the questioning began. "Binky, did you know the girl that got shot outside the Western Union?"

His facial expression changed, as he removed his hand. "Why you ask?"

" 'Cause the fuckin police came to my house! I leaned over close enough to feel his breath hit my face. "They think she was working for you. And they think you had something to do with her murder! Look at me Binky," I yelled. "She wore the same type of jacket you gave me!"

Binky pulled over to the side of the road, and tried to lay me down in the seat. I got scared, but kissed him back anyway. We started to grind, and groan, something terrible, but then I came to my senses.

"Binky, we've gotta talk first." I pushed him off of me. "What happened to the girl?"

"Kim, she was workin' for me, but she was workin'

for the police too. The police around here real slick. They got all kind of informants. My inside connection told me she was on her way to meet Rodriquez the night she got shot."

"Rodriquez?"

Binky nodded.

"That's one of the cops who came to my house. They're after you!"

"Yeah. I know. They've always been after me," he said without worry.

"How you know?"

"I've got connections. Money can buy anything, even members of the Raleigh P.D."

"So did you kill the girl?"

Binky sat dumbfounded.

"Binky if you expect for me to be loyal to you, then I expect the truth.

He rubbed the back of my head. "Kim, all that matters is that now she can't testify against me."

This was way too much for me to digest. I turned to look out the window as Binky started to drive again. I noticed we were in North Raleigh, where most of the *white folks* lived. The neighborhood was beautiful, and I wondered why we were out there, especially at one o'clock in the morning. The house that we stopped at was 'like that'. Slowly, we pulled in the driveway, close to the iron gate. After rolling down his window, Binky punched in a few numbers on the silver keypad that stood yards away from the gate.

Immediately, this white guy came stepping from an exit door within the gate, and said a few words to Binky that I could barely make out. Binky handed him a shoebox that he grabbed from beneath the seat. In return, he slid Binky three wads of money wrapped in thick rubber bands. He introduced us, and told him that I'd be in touch with him soon. My eyes popped out of my head.

"What do you mean, I'll be in touch with him soon?" I asked, once Binky backed away.

"This is someone you'll need to know later. 0833 is the code. He only gets a quarter at a time, but he's a regular and he's safe." He touched my arm to make sure I was still coherent. "That's $6,000. Ya follow me?"

"Uh huh." I nodded. "I'm just not sure why you're telling me this."

Hell, the thought of making $6,000 in one whop had me mesmerized. But, when Binky slid me my portion totaling $500, I woke the hell up.

"You might need to know this info later." Binky looked a bit stressed as he began to spill his guts. "Kim, it's just a matter of time before they take me in."

"I thought you said you had connections!"

"I do. That's how I know I've been under investigation for a while."

My anxiety increased as I listened to Binky fill me in on all the money he was making around Raleigh, and all his connections. I wondered if he had told Black Tye, or C-man any of this information?

"Kim, you ready to step up to the plate?" he asked pulling over about a quarter of a mile from my house.

"I guess."

Binky reached across me and opened the glove box. "Take this map," he said. "It'll lead you to my supply of coke."

"You gotta be kidding." I said looking at the map filled with country roads and a big red X Binky had marked with a red magic marker.

"Hopefully you won't need it. But if I get locked up, keep the business going. For now, I've got about twelve keys hidden at this spot. Ya follow me?"

"Got it." I recorded everything mentally. "What's the pig on here for?" I asked, out of curiosity. "The product is on a farm?"

"Kim, you're always thinkin' ahead." Binky placed his hand under his chin. He couldn't believe I was the same Kim. "Remember one important thing. If you run out of product, don't re-up on your own. That's where you'll get caught up. My connection can be trusted. But don't trust anyone else."

"Who's your connection?"

"Don't worry about that. If we ever need to resort to this plan, I'll be in touch somehow; even if it's in the visiting room." He smiled like this shit is a game.

I stuffed the map in my back pocket while analyzing

all that had been said during drug class 101. Binky spoke like he knew it was just a matter of time before he went down. And I was next in line.

***

Chapter 11

A week had gone by and I had been studying like hell. At 6:30 am, I had my books sprawled out on my bed trying to finish my homework for Ms. Porter's class. With my eyes heavy as sandbags, I wrote sloppily finishing the last few sentences. When the phone rang, I answered it on the first ring.

"Girl . . . . I ain't gonna keep roaming the streets with you every night. Shit, I'm tired," Rhonda whined.

I checked to make sure Momma wasn't eavesdropping. "I'm tired too, damn it! At least you had a few hours of sleep." I glanced at the clock. "I had to start my work once we came back in."

Even though Binky was still on the streets, he had decided to play a more inactive role. So, I had been making most of his runs late at night after Momma had gone to bed. The wear and tear on my body was becoming too much for me, but obviously killing Rhonda.

"I'm about to go back to sleep." Rhonda said. "Fuck school."

"I gotta go to school."

"The only thing you gotta do is drop my mothafuckin' money over here," she said, in a more serious tone.

"Rhonda don't play me," I snapped. "Don't I always pay you when I get paid?"

"Kim, things are different now. I know you handling the money," Rhonda replied. She began to laugh crazily. "Kim, you my girl. I'm just delirious from staying up 'til 3 a.m. every night with yo ass." She breathed heavily. "I'll see you in school later. I'ma catch me a few hours of sleep."

***

When I got to school, it was almost like Tee-Tee was waitin on me. Right outside my first period class, she stood with her arms folded. Tired as hell, I walked right up to her and shoved the palm of my hand in her face. "What do you want?" I asked. "'Cause I ain't feelin' no bull-shit today."

"Why do you keep telling people that Big Mike ain't my daddy? You don't know if he's my daddy or not. So you need to stop running your mouth," she fired!

"Look Tee-Tee, you keep bringing fake-ass pictures to school, and you're the one who keeps saying I'm your sista. Maybe you need to talk to your freak-ass momma. Maybe she might know who your father is, 'cause my momma knows who she sleeps with."

The bitch went crazy. She started screaming and yelling about her momma knows who she sleeps with, and that nobody disrespects her mother. She said that her daddy was with her momma first.

I went ballistic. I lunged at her, in an attempt to scare the bitch, but Tee- Tee was no slouch. She hit me with a left hook that landed firmly below my chin. I looked up at her like Sophia from the Color Purple. We started fighting like hell. I yanked her by the hair and pulled a big plug of her weave out of the top of her head.

Suddenly, Tee-Tee tackled me by the legs. I fell to the floor causing my new mini-skirt to fly in the air. As soon as the guys standing in the hallway got a glimpse of my black-laced panties, they cheered me on. "Whip that ho," they yelled. The attention she had brought to us, made me even madder.

We rolled from side to side, hitting, scratching, and yanking each other's hair. I knew if I could rip the weave from her scalp, she'd be finished. I got sidetracked when I turned to see Rhonda standing there. First of all, I didn't expect her to be in school. Secondly, she watched me roll on the floor as if she liked it. When Tee-Tee's spit landed on my face, I took extreme measures. I punched the hell out of her, knocked her front tooth loose, and was ready for more blood.

Finally, two of the teachers rushed over to pull us apart. There we stood bloody, bruised, and hair looking wild.

Once in the Principal's office, I made sure not to say a word. I watched Mr. Fox, pull our folders from the silver-plated file cabinet. He studied them carefully before speaking. "Kim Reynolds and Teresa Saunders," he said. "Ummm . . . Have we called the parents yet," he yelled from his office to the flighty secretary.

"They're on the way," she responded.

I sunk down in my chair. "The first chance I get to whip Tee-Tee's ass again, she's gettin' it," I thought. "I'm in enough trouble," I mumbled.

"Do you have something to say, Miss Reynolds?" asked Mr. Fox, as he glanced over his desk. "Because, you see, I'd love some answers!"

Tee-Tee stood up. "I was just trying to settle a few family issues. I'm tired of walking around knowing she's my sister. I was just trying to get the record straight. I was always taught family sticks together."

"Family my ass," I blurted sarcastically.

Mr. Fox's eyes lit up. This was more than he wanted to deal with. "How do you know she's your sister for sure?" he asked looking toward Tee-Tee.

Just then, my heart skipped a beat. Looking toward

the door, I couldn't believe my luck. How did you know to come?" I asked Big Mike.

"Tee-Tee's grandmother couldn't come, I happened to be in town, so she asked me to come."

I sat with a dumb look on my face. "So you're here for her," I asked with sadness in my voice. As my mother walked through the door, her stare told me that she wasn't surprised. I reared back in the chair, and placed my right hand under my bruised chin.

"Okay, this is the situation," Mr. Fox said to my parents. This seems more like a family matter rather than a school matter. I'm not sure how to resolve this, but here at school, they have to follow the rules." My parents nodded in agreement.

Mr. Fox rattled on about school rules and policy. In between his sermon, he asked me and Tee-Tee a few questions. My answers were short and to the point. Tee-Tee spilled her guts. She was really into her feelings about not having her mother around, and about wanting to have a good relationship with me. I wasn't having it. Her thinking that I could be a substitute for her mother was stupid anyway. The only time I responded was when Mr. Fox said, "Ten days of suspension will make her see the light."

Agitated, I yelled out. "So, how am I supposed to do my work, and graduate?"

"That's for you to figure out, young lady." Mr. Fox raised from his desk and escorted us all out. "So, are they really sisters," he asked.

"Yes," my father confirmed.

My momma pulled Big Mike to the side briefly before we headed to our car. She whispered something in his ear to make him frown.

Seeing Big Mike and Tee-Tee leave together, left a hole in my heart. It seemed like they shared a closeness that he and I never had. As soon as momma shut the door, and started the engine, I wasted no time. "How long have you known," I asked.

"Kim, I had my suspicions at the funeral. But Ms. Faye confirmed it a few weeks ago. First, I had to deal with the fact that y'all are about the same age." She looked away from me purposely. "I was trying to figure out a way to tell you."

I held my head down the rest of the way home. We rode in complete silence.

***

Later that night my runs for Binky went extra smooth. It was almost like hustling was therapy. Binky knew about my fight earlier with Tee-Tee. He encouraged me to make amends with her. He talked about his relationship with his brother, and how he trusted him more than anybody.

"So, why ain't you teaching him to handle your runs for you," I shot back.

"'Cause he ain't ready. He's not focused, and you are. But I bet if you tried to do me wrong, he'd handle you."

"Now, why would I ever do that," I said, stealing a wet kiss from Binky.

He smiled back at me as we pulled onto the lot at White's. The parking lot was bustling for one o'clock in the morning. I thought about telling Binky to come back later until I noticed the mysterious Cressida to my left.

Binky wasn't worried; he'd dealt with White for years. He told me to go on in, and handle things as usual. I moved in slow motion, walking inside. I could see the Dread watching my every step, just like I wanted him to. Inside White treated me like royalty. "How's my girl," he said, pulling me close. For a white-man, he had an extra-suave personality, to match perfectly with his magnetic cologne. *Luckily, he wasn't black, 'cause I might have to go at him.*

"Kim, I'll be with you in a moment," he said. "You know Stix, right."

"We've met." *Finally, I know his real name and can stop calling him Dread.*

While studying his permanently tanned, island skin, I extended my hand trying to show off my manners, when Stix's strong grip mesmerized me. He gripped my hand like he wanted to take me home right away. I glanced at his sculpted biceps when White spoke.

"I'll be right back," White said, leaving us standing

face-to-face.

"Me see you see again, pretty lady."

I blushed. Then turning to see if Binky could see me, I changed my demeanor.

"Tell me star," he said in a deep, Jamaican accent. "Binky say yuh not his woman. Me like a date wit' yuh star."

My jaw dropped. I looked out at the car hoping to get a glimpse at Binky. "A date? Sure," I said, wanting Binky to pay for his comment.

"Saturday night. Here's me number. Call me," he said.

White came from behind and handed Stix a key. "Thanks my man."

"No thank you," White replied. "Enjoy." He placed his hands back in his pocket like he'd proudly made a sale.

As soon as Stix was out the door, I started in on White. "He doing the same thing I'm doing," I asked, expecting the truth.

White laughed. "No . . . .. Kim. I'm in the business of selling cars, he's in the business like you- but his method is a little different."

I didn't want to appear stupid, so I played along. " Yeah, I know all about that."

He laughed. "It's just that he's got a different supplier. It's no offense to you," he said pinching my cheek. "You're my girl."

I smiled and removed the over-sized package, stuffed inside my pants. He grinned. "This is for you," he said. "As usual, it's all there."

Just then, Stix created a lot of noise, when he sped from the parking lot in a black-on-black 190 Benz. Followed by his boy in the Cressida. My eyes popped open wide when I noticed his custom-made spoiler kit with gold-plated BBS rims. I thought, *Now that nigga knows how to do things.* It was almost as if White read my mind.

"The boy is making money," White laughed wildly. "See, Kim, you make enough paper, you get whatever you want too."

"I ain't into flossin'." I lied. Binky was wearing off on me. But I was feelin' Stix and imagined me riding with him by next week.

"Oh, I almost forgot. Take this number," White said handing me a piece of paper.

"Who is it?" I asked.

"My boy, Dub. Call 'em. He needs some weight."

"Can he be trusted?"

"You know it. Just watch out for his dogs," White laughed hysterically.

"Thanks for the referral. I'm out."

***

Chapter 12

When the announcer behind the podium said, "Kim Reynolds," I almost blacked out. I couldn't believe I was really graduating. I had been sitting in a polyester, black cap and gown for hours listening to the speakers, and wondering if administration had made some mistake.

After being suspended, I figured Ms. Porter had gotten the best of me. Somehow between Momma turning in my work, and her prayers, this was real! As I walked across the stage, I could hear my mother yell, "You did it, Kim." She was so proud of me. Her hands clapped together so loudly everyone turned to get a glance at my number one fan.

I shook Mr. Fox's hand and grabbed my diploma as quickly as I could. I turned to find Chanel who had already walked across the stage, sitting in sadness. After motioning her with my hand several times, I gave up. She wasn't lookin' my way at all. Rhonda, who sat three chairs away from me, smiled like Tupac was coming to town. She wore black sunshades and popped gum the entire ceremony.

I guess the fact that C-man was there for *her* graduation, had her brain on swoll. It wasn't enough that she already thought highly of herself, but lately since dating C-man, Rhonda was out of control. For me- I didn't call what they were doing -dating, it was fuckin'.

The announcing of the cap turn, snapped me from my daze. We all screamed, "The Class of 1990," like we were really going on to bigger and better things. Family and friends immediately rushed us. In the center of the crowd, I moved my head from left to right searching for my mom. I was determined not to get sad, by looking for Binky. He said he'd be there, but I hadn't seen him. As a matter of fact, a lot of my phony supporters were missing, including Ms. Faye.

When I reached the end of the row, Chanel, Latisha, and Rhonda stood excitedly. I hugged Latisha first, as soon as I saw her face. It was my only connection to Binky. We hugged tightly, knowing that this was a major accomplishment for Southgate girls. Before we could loosen our embrace, the rest of the crew jumped in, and created the best huddle; I had felt in a while.

But to my left, I noticed my mom and dad exchanging puzzling looks. My father was dressed nicer than usual. His crisp linen suit looked tailor made, and complemented his extravagant jewels. "Congratulations Kim," he said, extending his arm with six, fresh long-stem roses.

I reached for the roses. "Thank you."

"Is that all I get?" Big Mike stood with his arms opened wide.

I smiled slightly, thinking about him being back in town permanently for over two weeks. *This was my first time seeing him.* Forgiveness was always one of my weaknesses, but now a proud graduate; why not give it a shot. I walked toward his embrace. But the sight of Tee-Tee stopped me dead in my tracks. Her face glistened from the sun. "Hello, Kim." Tee-Tee greeted me like nothing had ever happened between us.

Strangely, she resembled me more today, than ever before. People in attendance could've been fooled into thinking we were two happy sisters, both carrying roses from our father. At the same time, he grabbed us both, squeezing us tightly. I somewhat resisted.

"Kim, it's not my fault," Tee-Tee whispered softly. The passion in her voice startled me. I could tell she was serious about mending our relationship.

"You're right," I said, after shooting my father an unruly look. "Friends," I said, reaching out to give her some dap. My mother looked at me like I was crazy.

Tee-Tee extended her hand in a lady-like fashion. "Sisters," she said with a smile.

In the midst of the drama, I turned to see my crew making plans without me. C-man was in the center of the circle, surrounded by Latisha, Chanel, Black-Tye, and Rhonda. "Where are we celebrating?" he asked Rhonda, who was hanging over his arm, salivating like a German Shepard.

"Whatever you like," she said, imitating a scene from '*Coming to America.*'

"Now, this a down-ass girl," C-man bragged. "She wants what I want."

"I've gotta go pack," Chanel blurted out.

"What?" I yelled. My eyebrows twisted somewhere near my forehead.

My momma came to the rescue. "Yes, Chanel is leaving tomorrow. Her mother got the job. She starts next week."

My whole day was shot. There was no way I was hanging out with the crew, without my girl. "I'm going with you," I said to Chanel.

"I'm fine, Kim. Go celebrate," Chanel responded.

"Yeah, Chanel don't need no baby-sitter," Rhonda joked.

I spent the next thirty minutes walking around the field with Chanel, as the janitors dismantled the graduation set-up. While Momma and Ms. Willis talked secretly, I listened to Chanel tell me all that she'd been going through. I started to break down and cry, but had been molding myself into this hard-nosed rough neck.

When Chanel told me about the days when she's unable to even get out of the bed, I listened closely trying to figure out how I'd help her. The worst part was when she said; she might eventually end up in a wheelchair. I bit my lip to keep from crying.

***

An hour later, I found myself laid out across my bed with money scattered about. Lately, my stack had grown by leaps and bounds. I had been hustling every night from 1 am to 5 am. Strangely, my body had adjusted, and very little sleep was required. The money sprawled about was my motivation. $12,000, the latest total on my profit, had been growing like a newborn on cereal. The other $20,000 stacked to the side belonged to Binky.

I sat wondering how much longer we'd get paid. Chanel's comments flashed through my mind. *You're not going to do this forever, are you?* No, I didn't wanna become a professional hustler, but I was in too deep. Binky needed me.

Besides, Momma laid down the law a few days ago. She told me that college was not an option. My father agreed to pay for me to go to Wake Tech Community College, right here in Raleigh. They thought I'd make a great lawyer. *Hell, if he thinks I'm so great, somebody should send my ass to Howard. I bet I could rock D.C.*

College doesn't sound that bad, but would I make the same money, I'm making now? Hell, no! I rubbed my temples, disgusted at how my day was going. I thought about grabbing a couple of aspirin, when the phone rang.

"Hello." Short, hysterical huffs sounded. "Who is this?" I asked.

"Kim," a voice said in between breaths. "Turn . . . on . . . the . . . T.V."

I darted from my room, with the phone on my ear. I wanted to ask the female voice what channel, but the dial tone echoed. Four, five, seven, the channels flipped. *Nothing.*

Finally, channel nine was it! I sat frozen, trying to shake the disbelief. The words BREAKING NEWS was splattered across the screen. When my eyes zoomed in on Binky's mug shot, my face reddened. The footage showed several police vehicles, dogs, and Latisha crying in front of her house. Binky was taken out in handcuffs. He took it well, as opposed to C-Man and Latisha, who yelled at the officers. "Fuck all y'all bitches," she screamed. Officer Rodriguez was front and center, grinning as if he'd caught a mass murderer. Although their house was nothing to rave about, it was being seized on local TV.

The poised news reporter spoke like she was covering a white house event. "This is a victory for the Raleigh P.D.," she said proudly. *This is somebody's fuckin' life*, I thought. All of a sudden, I felt my body lose oxygen. I just knew my heart wouldn't make the next beat. *They might be comin' to my house next.*

I ran to my room, paced the floor for a second or two, and decided to stay put. I swooped the money from the bed, and bundled it back into the thick rubber bands.

I thought about how Binky would want me to handle this situation. Panicking wouldn't be his choice. I ran my fingers through my hair, and headed toward the kitchen with the money in hand. Opening each drawer with the speed of a bullet, I rambled through the mess in search of some tape. I knew if Momma saw me like this, she'd have me committed. "Got it!" I yelled.

Opening the broiler, near the bottom of the oven, my body turned upside down like the exorcist. Within minutes, the money was taped securely to the roof of the broiler. Feeling like I'd accomplished the first task of many, I squatted on the floor to think for a moment. *Every second counted.*

Back up again, I banged the wall! Pacing the floor, a shiver of fear raced through my body. *How would I handle everything alone? At least before, when I made runs, it was known that even though Binky wasn't there, he had my back. What am I thinking? I might be sharing a jail cell with Binky any day now.*

"A warrior handles anything," I repeated to myself, louder and louder. I ran to the back room, whipped out my composition book, and jotted down what needed to be taken care of; *collect money on the streets, get up with C-man, find a place for my money, go to Binky's hidden stash. Oh shit, Binky's stash.* I smirked nervously.

***

Chapter 13

With Binky gone, things weren't the same. I tried to contact C-man to get some insight on anything that wasn't known about Binky's operation. Unfortunately for me, word is, that C-man took Latisha and fled to a different state. Once their house got seized by the police, he couldn't trust anybody. As a matter of fact, our entire neighborhood was acting tricky. Black Tye couldn't even convince our trusty cabby to take us on our run. For days, I had bounced the idea back and forth of looking for Binky's supply on my own. But, without a license, or a car, I needed Tye.

Although rough around the edges, he was loyal. Binky could trust him, maybe not to be a leader, but protect him from danger. So now, he's my right hand, and my second pair of eyes. As instructed, Tye got us a loaner car from White's. At first he showed up in a 190 Benz, until I told him we needed something more low-key.

Everything was moving smoothly as planned until we reached the rural limits. Tye turned off on route 17 following my lead. I sat comfortably in the Camaro reading Binky's map like a champ. The only thing that still puzzled me was the picture of the pig. Suddenly, we came to a cross road that made no sense. I thought about asking Tye to help, until I noticed him bobbing his head, in conversation with himself.

I studied the map intensely, and then checked the route numbers posted on the pole. The sun had gone down and the area was getting darker by the minute. "Back up," I ordered. Tye wasted no time. Swiftly, he backed up going thirty. "Here. Turn here," I said hesitantly.

Tye whipped the corner, and we headed west for the next three miles.

"According to the map, it's somewhere around here," I said, slowing the pace of my voice.

"Nothing is here. Is the coke buried?"

"How the fuck would I know. Do you see this X?" I asked, shoving the map in his face.

Tye reduced his speed. He twitched in his seat. "This was a bad move," he said.

"Look, don't start that attention deficit shit on me!"

"You asked me to come!" he snapped.

"Sit back! I think that's it over there."

"Where?" Tye asked. "I'on see no pigs."

"That barn back there." I pointed several yards away from the highway. The small, feeble lookin' barn looked as if the roof had already caved halfway in, and was just waiting for us to finish the job.

Tye pulled off onto the side of the road, and hit the blinkers.

"Look, you retarded ass nigga, if the police comes by, they're gonna think we need help. Turn those damn blinkers off." I looked around for a better spot. "Pull off over there, behind those trees."

Finally, we had parked discretely, and made our way across the street. As soon as I took my first step into the tall grass, I wondered what the hell I was thinking. "A fuckin' barn," I yelled out. Tye paid me no attention. His hand was positioned on his .357. "You think we're going to a gun fight?" I asked. "Stupid mothafucker," I mumbled, after being ignored.

As we got closer, I stopped and caught my breath. I studied the grass praying no rodents, snakes, or sick lookin' creatures crawled on my new shoes. Tye kept moving, so I moved right behind him. When we got within a few feet of the barn, I knew it was the right spot because the image of a pig was drawn on the outside door.

"Damn, we need a flashlight," Tye shouted.

"Got it," I said, pulling out a small flashlight that I

borrowed from White's dealership. My anxiety increased ten notches when I shined the light around. The dim light from the outside created a reflection that kept me from seeing clearly. A soon as Tye shut the door slightly; my eyes caught the attention of a chest sitting in the corner of the barn.

"That's it." With the strength of a mule, I opened the raggedy chest without Tye's assistance. Instantly, I got nauseated lookin' at the perfectly bagged packs of cocaine. The thought of all of the responsibility that came with this coke was overwhelming.

"Here, gimme the bag." Tye cut in front of me.

"Where you think we gonna keep all this shit?" I questioned, with my hands riding my hips. "Binky kept it here for a reason, and so will we."

Tye had become antsy. He grinned, "How much we takin' for now."

"I don't want no bull-shit outta you," I spat. "You a little too happy. Binky didn't tell me to bring you out here. I brought you because I knew you always looked out for him. But don't get us locked up."

"Kim, I've been in this game longer than you!"

"Yeah, but Binky left *me* the map, and *me* the instructions." I threw Tye two packages and kept one in my hand. "We gotta hold it down until Binky gets out," I said shutting the chest.

"You don't even know how much is in each bag," Tye bragged.

"I'm smart enough to figure it out," I shot back.

Tye eased up a bit, sensing that I'd cut him from the plan. "There's a brick in every bag. You know kilo," he said sarcastically

"Nigga, I know," I snapped.

"If we sell all three of these, that's about seventy two thousand."

I smiled at the thought of selling out. "If the rest of this shit ends up missing, I guess Binky knows who to kill!" Tye was my boy, but I wanted to make sure we had an understanding.

***

Emotionally exhausted, I asked Tye to drop me off in front of Mr. Jack's store. We had successfully hidden the coke at Zandy's house. Now that she and Black Tye had made their relationship official, she was game. In so many words, I told the bitch, I'll kill her if anything ended up missing. Black Tye couldn't believe how I'd stepped up to the plate in just a few days.

When he dropped me off, I scrambled to fix my clothes, and hair, since I was right on schedule to meet Stix. Mr. Jack's store was our meeting spot. I called him yesterday attempting to cancel, but he insisted that we meet. He knew all about Binky's situation, but claimed that his misfortune should have no impact on us.

To my surprise, as I searched for Stix, I saw Momma

and Big Mike instead. My first thought was to keep moving down the street. But something didn't seem right. Momma's hand was moving back and forth like there was a problem. I sped my steps trying to inch toward her rescue. "That's right, I said it," I heard her say. "You seem to have money for everything else, but her."

Big Mike could barely look me in my face when I approached. He looked surprised as he swung a full set of keys back and forth below his knees. The keys looked familiar, I just couldn't make the connection. "Momma, you okay," I asked.

"Oh, I'm fine." She folded her arms. "Ms. Faye just told me some disturbing news about your father."

"What about me?" my dad hassled. "I'm straight."

"I'm sure you are," I added.

"He always has been. Now, even better than before," my mom interjected.

"Kim, I gotta proposition for you," he blurted out, as he saw Ms. Faye coming toward us.

"No thanks." I turned in search of Stix. I had to make my move before he pulled up in front of Momma. "I'll see y'all later," I said walking away.

I stopped in my tracks hearing my dad say, "Come work for me, here at the store."

Instantly, I turned, looked at the store, looked at my dad, and glanced down at Mr. Jack's keys, and swiftly moved away. *How did he become the owner of Mr. Jack's store*? I cringed.

"Not so fast missy," Ms. Faye said, grabbing me by the arm. "You and your daddy are in the hot seat."

My first instinct was to worry about what Ms. Faye had to say, but instead I scrutinized her outfit. She wasn't known to be the best dresser in the hood, but coming to the circle with pink and yellow hair rollers falling out of her head, wasn't her style. There was something different about Ms. Faye, but it went unnoticed because her mouth was flapped as usual.

"Leslie, I refuse to be labeled as a snitch. But this one, I've gotta tell." As she lit up her cigarette, I panicked. "Word on the street is that your daughter is slinging more drugs than ten hustlers put together."

"That's ridiculous." My mom glanced at my father to see his reaction. Her eyes revealed that she felt bad about not telling him when the officer's came to the house. "How sure are you?" she asked.

"One hundred percent. Do you think I just made this shit up?"

"Of course not." By now, Big Mike and Leslie stared at me like my sentence would be death row.

Big Mike cracked his knuckles. "Looks like you have some explaining to do."

"No, you do, 'cause I also heard, that you're the ring leader." Ms. Faye pointed directly in my dad's face. "You know what they say, *the apple don't fall far from the tree*!"

"Faye, have you been smoking," my mom asked. "I

don't believe a word of this. Just stop it right now."

"You don't have to believe me if you don't want to. He ain't gon' tell you the truth. He's lied about sending money, when he was coming to visit, how many extra children he had, so he'll lie about this too. Just another sad song!"

My mother's eyes showed that she did believe some of what Faye said, but her words were crisp. "I don't want to hear anymore!"

"Fine. Wait and hear it from the judge! Leslie you know damn well I told your ass Kim was doing too much in the streets. Stop letting that damn girl make a fool out your ass. I guess your prissy ass will believe it when she gets locked the hell up."

"Faye, you let me handle Kim if you don't mind."

"Her fuckin name is ringing bells in the streets, and you know I know what the hell I'm talking about. She ain't doing no different than her daddy, and your ass is still acting like Stevie Wonder."

Just then, the loud sounds coming from a distant caught everyone's attention. We knew it was music, but couldn't figure out where it was coming from. When I looked over my shoulder, I recognized the driver immediately. Driving a little below the speed limit, Stix hit the block with '*Flex, Time to Have Sex*,' pumping at top volume. He pulled right in front of the store, and frowned at the dirty looks my parents dished out.

I dropped my head and ran to the kitted out Benz,

hoping Stix would pull off before I got both feet in the door. He shocked the hell out of me when he leaned over my body, smashing my breast. I followed his mean gaze from my window. Surprisingly, it was directed at my father!

I squirmed in my seat noticing that Big Mike's stare was just as deadly. What in the hell was going on? At this point, I didn't even want to tell Stix that Big Mike was my father, or did he already know?

"What's the problem?" I asked, pretending that everything was okay.

"Stix continued to hold my body hostage as his muscular frame pressed against me. "That's supposed tuh be me store!" He pointed at what use to be Mr. Jack's store. "He blood clot don't deserve it!" he said spitefully.

My heart pounded. I thought about getting out when I saw my mother headed toward me. "Get out the car!" she yelled. Her voice sounded more stern than I'd ever heard.

My eyes met hers. "Pull off," I ordered.

Stix instantly pulled away from the curb going fifty. "What do you mean, that's supposed to be your store?" I asked, bothered by the situation.

"The bitch Donna still owes me money, mon. The agreement was that if she not pay me paper by last Friday, then this is me store, Star."

I tried to think of anything that would be in my dad's defense. "Well maybe she sold the spot to pay you in cash."

"Blood clot!" Stix bang his fist on the dash. He acted like he wanted to stab me. "I gave her a pass, when me allowed her to live. No she's playin' me. Plus how she gonna sell tuh me rival."

"Your rival. He can't be that bad."

"Yeah, Star. He da man dat 'ave good connect in de town. He's de only man who's gott a good connection in de town, other 'tan me. As a matta of fact, him sold tuh some of me folks before."

My mind raced. The man I thought I knew didn't exist. My father was obviously into something more than he could handle. Or could he? The man, who claimed to be broke, apparently had some cash. A part of me didn't want to believe it, but if he could be Stix's rival, then something was going on.

Stix's face grew angrier by the minute. "She'll get one blood clot bullet, mon, for every $10,000 she owes."

Calmly, my head nodded. I didn't give a fuck about Donna anyway. I never even been personally introduced to the bitch. But the fact that Stix spoke so bluntly had me caught between fear and excitement. "How much does she owe?" I asked hesitantly.

"Seventy-thou."

"Damn, I guess I'd be loading up the bullets too."

"Umgh." Stix cracked a slight smile for the first time since leaving my hood. "Yuh and bullets? Notta good match."

"Looks are deceiving," I replied.

"Show me yuh war marks and me show yuh mine," he said, in a more serious tone.

"I don't have any. That's how good I am." I laughed.

Stix frowned. Like a circus performer, he pulled his tightly fitted shirt over his head without missing a beat on the highway. Shocked, I hoped this wasn't the sign of date rape. When I looked up, most of the tension went away 'cause the sign above read *Crabtree Valley Mall.*

Before I knew it, Stix was showing off his many battle marks. From the cuts beneath his rib cage, to the old gun shot wounds that covered his arms; Stix wasn't to be played with. Strangely, I had the hots for the nigga; especially when I realized he knew how to treat a girl on the first date.

***

Chapter 14

My mother left me no other choice. After my direct defiance yesterday, I knew it was just a matter of time before we went toe-to-toe. She had already given specific instructions, ordering me to stay in the house unless I was looking for a summer job. *No can do*, I thought.

I knew she wouldn't understand, so I opted for the next best thing-*moving out.* Momma had always been good to me, and there were no complaints on my end. But this was my time to shine. Binky expected me to hold things down; and being on punishment wouldn't work. Although disappointed, she was actually willing to hear me out, until my father put his deceptive words in the mix.

I can't believe she would listen to anything he has to say. We struggled for years only to find out that he's been selling weight. Things escalated when I told Momma that Big Mike was the direct competition of a guy who sells hundreds of kilos a month. I didn't tell her that the competition was Stix. It shouldn't have mattered anyway,'cause she slapped the shit out of me when she found out, I was leaving for good. Still in all, on the way out the door, I hoped the $3,000 left on the counter would let her know that she'd always be good, as long as I'm living.

Dragging my suitcases out to the car, I had scary thoughts. Not because of the darkness that appeared from beneath my new Gucci shades, but realizing for the first time in my life, I was officially on my own. Even though Rhonda's house would be my lay over spot for now, Southgate was no longer my home. Rhonda had been calling all afternoon trying to figure out what time, I'd get there. She did her best to make me feel welcomed; she said Sam was even willing to give up his grimy room for a couple of nights. I smiled thinking about Rhonda's gesture, 'cause in general, she's a shady bitch.

When Tye saw me struggling, he stepped out to help me with my things. The bags were light compared to my wardrobe that was left behind. I figured between the new outfits Stix had sprung for and the new shit I'd buy for my new place, there was no need for used items. I looked back over my shoulder one last time. "Take me pass White's before we go to Rhonda's," I said shutting the door.

"Kim, you need your own spot." Tye frowned. "Nigga's gon' get green in a minute."

"Rhonda's cool," I responded. "Plus, she gon' work for us."

"That's the worst shit I heard all day." Tye looked at me like I wasn't capable of making good decisions. "You takin' money wit' you?"

"What else would I do wit it?" I lied with a straight face. Tye was my boy, but he didn't need to know where I kept all of the money. I just prayed momma would never have any reason to check the vents in the house. "I'm looking at a place over at Tara East apartments. It won't be ready until next week," I said.

Tye nodded, and turned up his sounds. Even though I'd heard, *Ain't Nothing but a G thang, by Snoop Dog* over a hundred times- today was the day that it became my anthem. A gangsta was what I'd become.

Twenty minutes later we pulled into Whites, and I jumped out like a pro. The new cars that had come in were freshly washed and showcased out front. A thought instantly crossed my mind about asking White how much I needed to get one. But my mind changed quickly after having a flashback of Binky's philosophy.

Walking in like the owner of the place, I waved at the workers in the lobby, and headed down the long hall toward White's private office. Over the last few days he'd given me the go ahead to come straight to the back. Just as I knocked three times with double knocks, White snatched the door open with a weird Jim Keri smile.

"How's my girl?"

I smiled. "I'm straight."

"You got something good for me," he asked, using his comical voice.

"As long as you got somethin' for me," I played along, as White locked the door behind me.

I liked White, but he made me think he was starting to smoke his own product. With no time to waste, I pulled a kilo from my new Gucci backpack-compliments of Stix, and tossed it on the table.

"That's for you," he said, admiring my tits. He pointed to a white bag.

I looked at the plastic bag filled with money. I thought about counting it in his office, like I'd been doing lately, but changed my mind quickly after taking note of the strange horny look on his face.

"It's all there? Right?"

"Of course," he said. "You know, I'd never short you. As a matter of fact, I buy more from you than I should, just to lay eyes on you." He laughed, moving closer.

"Is that right?" I asked nonchalantly.

Just as White put his hands on my shoulders, I opened the door. "Call me when you ready for more. I'm running low, but you first on the list."

"Oh, I got some custom cars that I think you'll like."

"I hope it that's 300 CE out front."

"No . . . I'm talking about something to help you

work better. A car with secret compartments."

"Secret compartments?"

"Yeah, we'll talk about it," he ended. "Can I get a kiss?"

"Hell no. I'll be in touch," I said, and shut the door.

***

Finally, we headed over to Rhonda's spot. I wanted to crash as soon as I hit the door. But the shit going on over here blew my mind as soon as my feet stepped inside. Niggas were playing cards in the corner, taking shots of liquor, hanging out at the back door, and people were coming in and out like roaches.

I kissed Ms. Jiles, and thanked her for letting me stay. "Make yo'self at home," she yelled, as she talked loudly with three women standing around the kitchen. "Sleep in that back room upstairs," she pointed.

I headed up the stairs and called out to Rhonda. "Rhonda!" I screamed, and got no answer. Sam walked out of Rhonda's room with his pants half zipped. "She's comin'," he said. "You sleeping in here."

I followed Sam as he took me to his old room. "I usually sleep with Rhonda," I blurted out.

"Yeah, but you'll be here a few weeks, so you need your own space."

When we got to my new sleeping quarters, first I had to squeeze between two guys drinking hen dog- and talking big shit. Then, after stumbling over two guys on the floor shooting craps, I paused at the harsh words. "Bitch, watch where you going," one of the guys roared. I had to pee so bad, I just said, "Fuck you," and dashed into the bathroom.

Coming out, I made my way back to my little space, and sat down on the smallest unmade twin bed, I had ever been on. I looked all around and viewed the piles of mess all around me. I was thankful for the invite from Rhonda, but damn, the paint was peeling and the room smelled like pee. Spending a night with Rhonda here and there had been a breeze, but this is on another level.

I peeped out the door, and shut it tight. As soon as the coast was clear, I flipped the worn mattress, to stash my money. Knowing it was a good spot settled my mind. My timing was perfect because Rhonda stuck her head in the door to check on me, just as I was sitting down. "You straight?" she asked.

"I'm fine," I said massaging the back of my neck. "I'm just tired."

"Call it a night," she said. "It's almost one o'clock."

"I can't tell." We both giggled at the fact that her house was like Grand Central Station.

As soon as Rhonda shut the door, I lifted the mattress one last time, hoping she had not seen me put my money there. I sat momentarily trying to relax and reflect on the day's events. But by the time I hung my gold rope, on the lampshade, sleep was a must. An hour or so later the noise had lessened and I was fast asleep.

***

I tried to wake up from my life-threatening dream. Lying in an unconscious state, I heard heavy footsteps that sounded like a herd of cows, stampeding in my direction. The steps became noisier by the second. Before I had a chance to react, my door came tumbling down. Coming through the door were two tall guys with black hooded sweatshirts, and black boots carrying nine's. They hit me with the gun, and I fell across the bed grabbing my face. With a sock slammed into my mouth, my eyes popped wide open. I struggled to hold my head up, when I felt cold hard metal against my back.

Quickly, I glanced at the broken lampshade and saw my gold chain still dangling. Lying on the dusty dresser was my 24 carat three finger ring, and my Gucci shades. Everything was still in place. *What do they wan* ? I wondered. I just knew they would grab my purse. No sooner than the thought left my mind, they tossed me aside, flipped the mattress off the bed and grabbed my money. I thought, *damn they went straight to my stash!*

They rushed out of the room firing wild shots in the air, daring anyone to move. Of course by this time, people in the house were just realizing what had happened, because it all went down so fast.

I gathered as much strength as I could, ready to chase

what was mine. Just then, Sam appeared at the door. Stunned, he held his hand out. "It ain't worth your life, Kim."

I stood speechless, with the mattress turned up side down near my feet. Rhonda screamed, "Kim, you alright," rushing to my side. I wanted to cry, but vowed not to. My gaze shifted from Sam to Rhonda, then from Rhonda to Sam.

I grabbed my bag wanting to punch Rhonda in the face. "Where you going?" she asked. "You safer in the house."

I gritted like a pit-bull. "I'll be back," I said.

There was a long pause. "Kim, you just got attacked, and now you wanna go out into the streets at four o'clock in the morning?" Rhonda crossed her arms like she wanted answers. "Are you stupid?"

"Not at all." I spoke my words slowly making sure Rhonda understood each word. I really didn't want to stay at Rhonda's anymore, but had no other choice. But for now, I could at least get some air till' morning. "I'll be back in a bit," I said, walking out of the room.

***

My head throbbed as I roamed the streets looking for Roc. Hopefully, he would remember me, and sell me some protection. After walking the streets all night and collecting some money from some runners, I needed a bath, but most importantly *a gun.* I couldn't believe I got jacked for my money. It couldn't be proven, but my gut feeling said Rhonda was guilty. She got me once, but the next time, she'd get a shock.

I knew I'd have to go back to Rhonda's because there was nowhere else for me to stay. The last time the leasing agent contacted me about my place; she said it would at least be another 10-12 days before I could move in. Plus, she said the first six months must be paid in advance due to my lack of credit. I needed to round up some more money.

Rolling up on a group of youngsters, I looked at them with a straight face. In turn, they watched me closely. I looked around until I spotted the exact same spot where I'd first met Roc. I headed in that direction. "Anybody know where Roc at?" I asked.

"Who the fuck is asking?" a skinny, thuggish guy said.

Just then, Roc's huge frame appeared from behind the abandoned apartment building. His left hand rested deep inside his pants.

"Hey remember me?" I didn't crack a smile.

"Sorta," he said, giving me an x-ray with his eyes. "What you need?"

"Binky told you, I'd be back." My eyes checked the area around me. "I need protection," I finally said.

"How much you got?"

"How much do I need?" I snapped. Reaching into

my purse, I pulled out a miniature bankroll.

Roc grinned. "You gotta pop somebody, or is it for, *just in case.*"

"Look, I can't handle the investigation right now. I just got robbed, so can you help me or not?" I stood with my hands on my hips waiting for a response.

"I'll be back with the steel. Have my mothafuckin' money," he said with a slight attitude.

I waited patiently as crack-heads roamed the area like I was the target for another robbery. Being worried was the farthest thing from my mind, because somebody would get fucked up for playin' with me right now. I stayed calm as a police car pulled to the left of me. "You got some kinda' trouble Miss," the slim officer asked while stopping completely.

"No, Sir," I replied.

He paused. "You sure?" he asked a second time. His look said it all. He couldn't figure out why someone dressed in all white linen would be hanging out on this block.

"I'm taking my cousin back home to Wendell-where it's safe," I lied with a smirk.

He nodded with approval. "Be careful," the officer said as he pulled off.

Just then Roc appeared from the back of the run down building. "Follow me." He nodded in my direction.

Once out of sight, Roc transformed into a

businessman. "Three hundred," he said. "No bodies." He waved a black nine-millimeter in my face.

"I'll take it." As soon as the exchange had been made, a smile slipped through my lips. *Now let's see what happens to the next mothafucker who comes at me wrong!*

***

Chapter 15

Sitting in the backseat of the loaner, I was a bit fucked up by the recent events. *I can't believe that Rhonda would jack me for my money. I gotta to get a strategic plan ready to get back on my feet. Not to mention, getting my own place and getting my own ride.* Admiring the nice houses on the drive, I noticed that we we're drawing near. "Pull up to the house on the left with the iron gate, and I'll run in!"

"So you think you stuntin' huh?" Black Tye giggled He pulled up hesitantly to the iron gate. I jumped out, turned to him and flashed my nine millimeter. Wearing a devilish smile, I said, "Lay low. I'm fixing to make this move."

I ran to the security panel and entered the code 0833. As I walked through the gate, I reflected on the instructions Binky gave me the night he handed over the map. Walking up to the white guy, I reached into my duffel bag and handed him a shoebox the same way Binky had. Taking the money, I stuffed it in my bag and handed him a pager number to get in touch with me. The older gentleman barely wanted to look at me. I wasn't trippin' cause he had Binky the same way. As long as the cash was coming in, it was fine with me.

***

Getting back in the car, *I thought, I should get a stash spot for my money.* I instructed Black Tye to go to the First Union Bank near Crabtree Valley Mall. *I figured that was the best way to go, so if shit ever hit the fan, the money wouldn't be traceable. Besides, I can't trust a damn soul and I don't wanna have to bus a cap in nobody's ass for fuckin' with my money.* As we entered the parking lot of the bank, I made sure to check my surroundings, just as I had done so many times before. I had learned from Binky that you never know who is watching. Sitting in the bank waiting for my name to be called, I looked around and saw a mother and her teenage daughter. For a minute, I got sad thinking *about my mom and how our relationship was going sour.* My trance was broken when they called my name and instructed me to walk to the back of the bank where the safe deposit boxes were. Hearing the gate slam *made me think about Binky and what he's going through in the joint. I know that I don't want to experience that shit.* I opened the assigned box, placed 5g's inside and the rest in my MCM bag that I copped when I went shopping with Stix. Mission accomplished.

***

Hopping back in the car, I told Tye, "We have a few more stops to make and then after that, take me to Rhonda's crib." We drove on to Maple Street by the basketball court and pulled right up in front. This young teenager walked over to the car and I handed him three bags. He looked at the bag and said, "Hey, what's up with that new shit?"

Aggravated because I didn't know what new shit he was talking about, I frowned my face at him. "What new shit? This is the same product you got when Binky came through. I know you ain't trying me?"

He could tell by the look Black Tye shot him, that he better clear this shit up and quick. "Naw Shawdy, I talkin bout dat crack." The excitement in his voice let me know this was something I needed to look into. Now that I'm in charge, I can't let my workers think they are one up on me, so I got to stay up.

"People have been coming through wanting that huh? I'm going to see what I can get my hands on, and get back with you on that. I will be back tomorrow to collect."

"A'ight, I'll see you." Driving away from the curb *I wondered* h*ow much money this crack stuff could bring.* I thought about it more and more as we covered every hot spot in Raleigh until all the runs were done.

***

"Tye, pull over, I need to use the payphone, my pager is blowing up." I smiled looking down at Stix's number. *Dude is really sweatin' a sista.*

"You need a cell phone."

"Nah, Binky said it's traceable."

We pulled up to a convenience store and I hopped out to use the phone. "Whats up?"

"Pretty Lady, me need tuh see yuh," Stix said in his heavy Jamaican accent.

"Pick me up at Rhonda's in an hour so we can go to the Waffle House." "A'ight, cool." I noticed Black Tye watching me intensely as I finished up my phone call. He was probably admiring how gangsta I had become in just a weeks time, or wondering who the hell could be blowing up my damn pager like that. Getting back in the car, I told him to take me to Rhonda's house. Reaching in my purse, I broke him off 5 crisp $100 bills. "I will call you tomorrow so that we can hook up and make a few moves."

"Bet," Tye responded satisfied with the payment I

had given him. He never made eye contact as he rocked to the loud sounds coming through his headphones. As I headed into Rhonda's place, I started thinking *that was a real power play with Tye.* It was important for me to make good payments with Black Tye, if I was gonna gain mad respect and his loyalty while Binky was away. Besides, I knew that Binky wasn't breaking him off with dough like that. Yeah, I was running the show now and it was crucial that Tye understood that. I walked into Rhonda's feelin on top.

As I got out of the shower and changed my clothes, I glanced at Rhonda thinking, damn, she's probably wondering how much money I made today? "Kim, when are you going to give me more work, I haven't been on a run since Binky's been gone. My money is getting low and I need some ends."

I know this bitch ain't trying to play me. First she stick me for my papers and now she trying to act like she broke. I should beat her down for playing with me. Wait 'til I get me a spot, I got something for her grimy ass. "I should have something for you soon." I turned to the mirror as I put the finishing touches on my outfit preparing to walk out the door.

Rhonda took notice to my gat on my hip and said, "I see you strapped". I looked her in the eye with an icy stare. "Yeah, when I find out the trick that took my money, Rock a bye baby. Hoping that I had instilled fear in her, I left the room.

***

Within minutes, Stix and I were on our way to grub out at the Waffle House. Singing along with Jodeci, "Baby won't you just stay, for a little while," Stix turned to me and asked "Yuh stayin' wit' me tunight?"

Hanging out with Stix had become a daily routine, but I was taken aback by the idea of staying with him all-night, and waking up next to him in the morning. "Can you take me to see my girl Chanel in Durham tomorrow?"

With a quizzical look in his eyes, he said, "Sure, anyting for yuh luv." "Anything?" *Thinking to myself that this would be the perfect opportunity to inquire about his money making, I said,* "I been down with Binky for a while and he ain't made no paper like what you getting."

Not sure if he could really trust me yet, Stix glared at me before answering. "What tis it about yuh, Star, me 'ave fallen for? Maybe it's those huge tits, that's makin' me need yuh on me team." He paused, looked me straight in the eye and answered. "Crack tis where it's at, Star; dat powder shit yis slow money, mon."

Crack! This dude really knows how this business works and I'm definitely ready to learn how to get this money. I gotta to play my cards right to learn as much as I can from this Rasta. Pondering on my thoughts we got out of the car to get our grub on.

***

On the ride over to Stix's place, we continued to make small talk, playing mind games on each other, and rocking to the sounds of Bob Marley. As the car started to slow down, I took notice of my surroundings as I had been taught to do. Stix's neighborhood was nothing like I had imagined it would be. He lived in the straight up ghetto. Hell, I thought, *Damn, this dude's hood is worst than the one I grew up in. I hope the inside is nice.*

As we entered Stick's place, the inside made up for what I had experienced on the outside. The joint was 'like that', especially his bedroom. He had a king sized waterbed with floor to ceiling mirrors covering the entire room. In one corner was a huge sound system and a theater vision system on the other wall. He even had a shag rug with a picture of the continent of Africa in black, green and red on the floor.

I sat down on the waterbed, and started bouncing up and down trying to fill the waves, and hear the splish splash sounds. I could hear him talking on his cellular phone. I couldn't make out the conversation, but I could tell that he was giving instructions from the tone of his voice. Even though I hadn't known him long, I realized that his Jamaican accent gets really thick when he gets excited; It was actually turning me on. At that moment, I began to think d*amn, I really miss Binky. But I gotta make this paper.* With Binky off the streets, I knew that Stix would be the only key to me being on top.

My thoughts were interrupted when Stix entered the

room. "Sexy, would yuh like sometin' more comfortable tuh slip into?" he asked, as he stroked my leg. *His touch made me tingle, I am really starting to dig this dude.* I looked at him with a sheepish smile. "I'll take a t-shirt".

As we laid across the bed, watching t.v., I figured that I should make the first move, so that he wouldn't look at me like a little girl. Running my fingers through his dreads I turned his face to me, and pulled him in for a wet, sloppy kiss. He moaned, and pulled me on top of him as we grinded in unison. I straddled him like I'd done this many times before.

Feeling his dick throbbing against my thigh turned me on. Rolling over on my back he lifted the t-shirt and cupped both of my tits, and nibbled on my neck. He made his way down, took in my hard nipple, and sucked it gently. "Yuh like that," he asked in a soft caring whisper."

I just moaned. *This was far better already than my experience with Binky.* He slid his finger in my moistness and teased my clit with his thumb. I had never felt so good in my life. *So this is what it's suppose to be like.* I closed my eyes and enjoyed what he was doing to me. So that he wouldn't think I was wet behind the ears, I stepped my game up, and started following his lead. I grabbed his manhood, and thought, *damn I need both hands to palm this thing. What in hell did they feed him growing up? Rhonda didn't tell me these things come in extra large.*

After kissing for what seemed like an hour, I braced myself for his entry. Unlike my first sexual experience he slowly eased himself in, inch by inch. "Let me know if it hurt baby. Me want you to enjoy me," he said as he licked my ear. Wiggling my hips, I was determined to take the pain and please him. The feeling of pleasure and pain combined felt good; squeezing him tight I opened my legs wider and welcomed him inside. Before I knew it we were both moaning and humping with sweat dripping everywhere. "Lay on your back" I demanded as if I was one of the girls on those x-rated movies. *I got to show him I am ready for him, to keep him in my corner.* I sat on his glory and rode him until I felt his body shake; it felt so good, I forgot all about protection, until I felt myself collapse on him. He grabbed me tight. "Me like 'tat, Star!" he whispered pecking my forehead.

"I think I'm falling for you Daddy." I knew I wasn't supposed to let him hit, that quick. I was kinda disappointed in myself. *Oh well, a girls got to do what a girl got to do.*

***

I woke up before dawn to go to the bathroom, not noticing Stix was not in the bed. I heard some noise coming from the kitchen. Standing in the kitchen doorway, I watched as it appeared he was baking a cake. I walked up behind him and hugged him around the waist. "What are you doing? It's 5 am." "Cooking up coke. Turning it into crack form." I watched him like I was in a chemistry class. I took notes on each step, as he instructed me to always use Pyrex to get the best results. As he got to the last key, he had me try my hand while he provided instruction. I measured meticulously, as he made sure I did just as he did. "Okay, let me check it, Star." He put the brick on his scale and looked closely. "It came back 80%. Good job for your first time."

I didn't quite understand what that meant, but I could tell from the expression on his face that I was a good pupil and had passed the test. "So what do you do with it now?"

"Sell it like this, or you can cut it into eight balls, and fifty's, and sell to the crack heads. Come on back to bed, you need your beauty rest." He grabbed my hand and led me back to the bedroom. As we walked toward the back, Stix made his move for round two.

***

I woke up to the smell of steak and eggs. When I popped my eyes open, there he was standing over me with a plate and a smile on his face. "You didn't have to do this". I sat up in the bed.

"Me gotta feed me lady." I ignored his comment, ate my food, showered and we were on our way.

On the ride to Chanel's I sat in the passenger seat,

staring at the green, yellow and black flag hanging in his window. While he handled his business on the phone, I listened carefully. "Look tell de bumbaclot, the best I can do is 30 g's for a brick," he spat in his cellular phone. Thirty *thousand! I can't believe this shit goes for that much. This dude is 'like that'. He taught me how to cook the shit up, fucked me good, and fed me in bed. Instantly, I thought about cooking up a few packs from the stash. I'm about to blow up.*

"What yuh grinnin' 'bout, Star?" Stix asked, as he put the car in park. He leaned over close enough to feel my breath.

"Thinking about you." *I love the attention he gives me when I am with him.* "Can you pick me up from here in the morning? I wanna spend some extra time with my girl, Chanel."

"Reach me later when yuh ready." I kissed him and jumped out the car.

***

Chapter 16

Laying back, chilling in the Benz, I reflected on my crazy life. Talk about up and downs- *I go from trying to make ends meet, to falling for a man who's now locked up, to getting' paid off cocaine, to now fuckin' with a paid Jamaican.* "Umh," I mumbled to myself.

Stix shot me a strange look, just as he turned up *Shabba Ranks* loud as hell. When we got closer to St. Aug.'s campus, Stix turned onto Addison Place, a known crack block. He cupped my face and blessed me with his tongue. "Me be back, Star."

I asked him in a sexy tone, "Are you gonna be long?"

"Me jus cum for me paper," he said, without looking me in the eye.

I looked at him and smiled. He had no idea how he'd entered my life at the perfect moment.

Before I knew it, Stix had gone into the raggedy house and closed the door.

Damn, I thought, *Addison Place is rockin'*. A different flashy ride passed me every other minute. My neck jerked back and forth watching the drug boys, and the money potential. *I just might need to ride back over here myself, I thought.*

I turned around for another look, when out of the back window, I see Ms. Faye. It took a minute to focus in on her frail body, trying to make sure I wasn't tripping. *What the hell is she looking like, wearing a crazy looking scarf, and some fuckin' furry bed-room slippers*? Her ass is far away from our block, and had no reason to be hanging on a crack block.

Even though Faye stood about five yards away, I leaped out the car and yelled her name. "Faye, Ms. Faye!" I looked real un-cool to the people on the block, but I waved my hand crazily, trying to get her attention anyway.

I couldn't believe Ms. Faye walked up and down the block ignoring me. I watched her as her hands rubbed back and forth over her hair, and she scratched her forearms at a steady pace.

When I heard a stringy head woman walk by saying, "You don't wanna fuck with Faye, she ain't no joke", it all clicked for me. *It's true*, I thought. These people know her.

Stixs, finally walked out of the house with a small

Newport duffel bag, swinging in his hand. "What me wifey doing out de car?" he asked with a frown.

"I'm a grown ass woman," I said.

"But you me blood clot woman."

I wanted to be happy about his comment, but my eyes stayed fixed on Ms. Faye as I got back in the car.

I straightened up in my seat when Stix threw his money bag on my lap. "That's thirteen thousand, Star, " he grinned devilishy. "Easy money, mon."

Still in my trance, I didn't comment. Ms. Faye looked like she was actually starting to sing a 'rap' song. Her head bobbed to the imaginary beats, as she stood on the sidewalk alone. Stix began to pull off when I stopped him.

"You see that woman over there," I said.

"The one snapping the fingers." Stix stopped in the middle of the street.

"Yeah. Am I tripping, or is she on that New Jack City shit?"

"Star, she's on it," he said, fixing his flag dangling from the rear view mirror.

I pushed Stix's shoulder slightly. Don't be so unconcerned. This is serious." I rolled the window down for a closer look. "She's been a family friend for years. Damn, I gotta tell my mama this shit."

"Star, yuh told me yuh mother don't talk no more." Stix's brow creased.

"She'll talk. This is important. Take me there!" I

pointed.

Stix looked at me strangely.

"Please . . . ." I begged.

***

Twenty minutes later, we arrived at my mother's house. "Hurry luv, me need some lovin," Stix said, gripping my thigh.

"It'll just be a moment." *Damn, I must've turned this nigga out. All of a sudden he wanting it, two, three times a day!*

It felt funny coming back to Southgate. Many memories flashed through my mind as I got closer to the front door. From a distance, I could see a piece of paper taped to the peep hole. Damn, I thought. *Momma must not be home.* But nothing could prepare me for what I saw.

I speed read the big yellow sign on the door. My heart dropped, realizing it was an eviction notice. "What the fuck!" I said to myself . . . "I gave Momma money to pay the rent . . . What did she do with the money?"

Frantically, I knocked hard enough to hurt my knuckles, but got no answer. My instinct told me to search for my key. In between my searching, I thought all kinds of bad thoughts. Was momma on crack like Ms. Faye? Had she lost her job?

Suddenly I found my key. But when I stuck it in the

hole, it didn't fit. Fucked up, I scrambled through my bag again, hoping that it was the wrong key. At this point I was in denial, because in my heart, I knew that was the right key. Out of the blue, a shadow reflected from behind me. "What do you want, Kim?" Momma asked, annoyed by my presence.

"Where is the money I left for you?" I held my palms o wide open, showing her I couldn't understand the note.

She stood in silence before speaking. "I never spent it, but it burned well."

Each word she spoke, hurt me to my bones. But I sucked it up. "Where you gonna live?"

"I'll live in the street before I take your dirty money," she snapped.

"I can't believe you Momma!" I wanted to cry. "I tried to make it for the both of us. You need money for your bills!" I scrambled through my bag searching for money. Three hundreds lay in the bottom of my purse. "Here," I said reaching toward her with the bills in hand.

"Hell no!" she yelled, slapping my hand away. The money fell to the ground.

"Oh, so now you cursing? Stop acting like Big Mike done hooked you up on some cash. You need to stop all that tripping and pay these damn bills around here."

My mother stared at me like a stranger.

I broke our hostile stare by telling her about Faye. "Did you know your good friend is smoking crack?"

"Kim, you come running over here telling me about something that I already know. Be concerned about yourself. I didn't teach you to be in the streets." She shook her head. "Don't come back over here, or call me until you change your life!" Momma quickly stuck her key in the door, opened it, and slammed the door in my face.

***

Chapter 17

It's move-out day and I'm hyped up. Shit was getting sticky at Rhonda's, so I openly accepted Stix's invite to move in with him. Someone stealing my loot got me pissed off. So pissed, I was geared up to pop anybody—including Rhonda's grandma if anything else of mine was missing. I got up before the sun, threw my shit in my bag, and jetted. Tiptoeing through the house, I thought, *damn once again, they're packed like sardines up in this crib.* Poor could not describe their level of desperation. I felt kind of bad for 'em. Rhonda's little sisters were raggedy as all hell, so I left a few items they could sport: an MCM backpack, a few pair of Guess jeans, some Levi's, and three pair of Nike's-never worn. On the other side of the door, the engine revved. My new man was waitin' on me. I jumped from the top porch step. By the time my feet hit the pavement, I couldn't help but move my ass to the rhythms of Shabba Ranks.

"Yo, turn the volume down, you gonna wake the dead," I said throwing my bags in the back seat. Stix gave me a killer Jamaican stare.

"Me feelin' it, Star. Nuh bodda me!" *Oh, I'll bother you all right. Shit, keep it up and this whip will be mine too.* I had to take a minute to laugh at my own ass for thinking that, 'cause I ain't that damn hyped to fuck wit his crazy Jamaican ass. I smiled and gave him a kiss. He took it with no emotion. Stix shot off leaving only dust in the wind.

We weaved in and out of traffic like we were running from 5.0. About thirty minutes down the Beltline, I turned the music down so we could talk. Stix eyes followed my hands to his kitted out sound system. He didn't say two words. I pumped the volume back up, even louder this time, slightly reclined my chair and enjoyed the ride. *This was a far cry from screwing with Binky's ass,* I thought. *The dick was better and the money.*

As we pulled up in front of a large brick home in a tight community, Stix turned the music off. "I thought we we're going back to your place?" I asked wondering where we were.

"This is me place. De othda place is where me work from. You neva shit where you eat," Stix said, without a smile.

I fixed my eyes on every detail. I couldn't believe that grass could be so green. I thought I'd died and gone to heaven. Hell, I had moved on up to the East Side.

He lived amongst some upscale Black folks in his neighborhood. I wasn't used to no quiet shit like this. *Damn I've arrived.*

"No company out here. Got it?" Every now and then Stix spoke that traditional Jamaican shit. But when he needed me to truly feel what he was sayin', he spoke my language.

I grabbed my bags. "Got it!" I walked toward the large oak door. I was so pressed to finally be with a good man, and on my own, I was willing to do just about whatever it took to make him happy. Hell, if he wanted me to, I'd knock off a couple of his damn babies. Shit who am I foolin' I got paper to chase. And ain't no dick or babies gonna stop that. I was determined to get rich or die tryin'.

As nice as his neighborhood was, the inside of his house looked like something right out the damn islands. All this color and shit made me need a pair of damn sunglasses. It was like someone farted a box of Skittles everywhere. I sat my bags down on the pink and green floral couch, and walked over to the pictures hanging above the mantel. "Who this, your mother?"

"Yuh too fass, relax."

"Well, is it?" Stix shook his head. "Yuh mon." He turned and headed for the kitchen.

"All a dem me family."

His little sister had some ashy knees. Where was the damn lotion? Lard, Vaseline or something, shit! Stix broke my concentration.

"Yuh wanta tall glass a wata?"

"Please," I said picking up a mask that reminded me of some voodoo object.

"Take yuh time before yuh break." *I needed to break it. That shit was spooky.*

Stix handed me the glass of water and turned to pick up my bags. "I need to handle some business around the way in a few hours."

He nodded and headed for the stairs. Minutes later he came back with a book in his hand. Stix threw the driving manual in my lap. I smirked.

"What is this for?" I asked.

"Me can't be your taxi, mon. It's time yuh get yuh license, so yuh can 'ave yuh own car." I like it when he takes charge. "I know how to drive already. My aunt Joyce used to let me drive her around every summer." He shot me a look. "Okay, you're right, I'll make it legit. Give me a week and I'll have it." I knew I was gonna get it in less than that, since word on the street, said Stix bought his women cars. Stix watched me as if to say, your ass better or you'll be stuck without a way here.

***

The next day, I paged Tye, and he took his time hittin' me back. "Why you got me waitin'?" I screamed in the phone.

"Look, I'm chillin' with one of my homies."

I moved the phone away from my ear. I checked the receiver to make sure I was in the right place.

"Nigga, chillin'? You know we got a job to do. Apparently you don't want your cut." Black Tye sounded a long huff through the phone.

"I 'ont want no setbacks," I said, before slamming the phone down. For some reason, Tye was gettin' real sloppy. He was pissing me off, acting dumb and shit.

We met behind Nash Square across from the Western Union. I told him to be there not a minute past ten, or else. We had to deliver some product to these connects over on Departure Drive. I wasn't used to operating with dealers who worked out of small distribution sites, but I had to do what I had to do. Me and Tye made sure we were both strapped.

The entire time we drove, he was actin' more unusual than ever—like he wasn't on his game, real nonchalant and shit. Time after time, I asked him a question and his ass answered with a nod, even though it wasn't even a yes or no question. The whole time, he never gave me eye contact.

"Is you high?" I finally asked out of frustration. I guess Tye got tired of hearing my voice, cause after that, he turned up his headphones. Now ain't that a bitch? I couldn't deal with his attitude right then. I had to get my head together for this transaction. This was my first time meeting Dub, but I was thankful White turned me on to him.

We pulled up in front of the location. Six pit bulls guarded the abandoned building. "Yo I ain't gettin' out," Tye said. *When did his ass start deciding what he wasn't gonna do?* I almost smacked them headphones off his ears.

"Nigga, you strapped, right? Shoot them bastards if you have to. Let's roll." I hopped from the car ready for action.

"Watch my back, fool." I surveyed the abandoned block for any funny business. Two steps toward the dogs, I yelled, "Pablo." The dogs fell back, and Black Tye's mouth dropped. I punched in the code as instructed, knocked three times and a Hulk Hogan looking dude, wearing a red bandana opened the door. He never said a word. He nodded his head in the direction we should go. The long dark hallway took us through a maze. When we passed through the elevator doors, Dub was standing at a wooden table with my cash.

"Count my money," I told Black Tye throwing him the duffel.

"It's all there," Dub said cutting open the package with a sharp knife. He tasted the product and smiled. "This is some good shit. I'll call you when I need to re-up."

Damn this was the last package I had stashed at Tye's girl, Zandy's house. I thought about the fact that there was only three more left at the barn. What the hell am I gonna do?

"Yo, you move crack?" Dub asked, breaking my concentration. I told him I'd have some by next week.

I looked over my shoulder to get the okay from Tye. He nodded. "It's all here." I took the bag and headed towards the door.

"Check you later," I said to Dub.

"Have that crack when you come back," he said firmly.

"Oh the entrance code will change on your next visit. The old shit will get you mauled." I shook my head and motioned for Black Tye to follow. I didn't appreciate the look he shot my way. *He's a dumb motha . . . .*

"Drive off," I told him as we got in the car.

He had the nerve to try asking me some damn questions about Dub, now it was my turn to just straight ignore him. I tuned his ass right out.

***

The next day, I was scheduled to pay Bink a visit. *What the hell was this,* I thought. The C.O.'s moved us through the halls like we were inmates. All this yelling and screaming about where to go and what to do, I wasn't feelin' any of it. They checked every part of my body. This ugly ass manly lookin' female cop told me to unhook my bra. "Open your pants and drop'em," she yelled.

"What?" I asked.

She gazed at my ass, as if to say, you heard what I said. I felt molested when she rubbed her hands around my panties. I was forced to take off my shoes and all my jewelry to pass through the mental detector.

After the humiliation, I was led into this room filled with green jumpers. I watched for some sign of Binky. He was all the way in the back at the last table. I practically ran with open arms, but he didn't budge.

"Sit down," he said, "I need to get at you on some serious business." I felt like my father was waiting to serve up a damn punishment.

"Well hello to you to," I said, with an attitude. *Shit I was running things now. Who in the hell did he think he was talkin' to?*

"So, how you makin' out," I asked. I figured small talk would work before laying it on Binky.

"I'm a'ight. I see you doing fine," he said making reference to my chain.

"Look, I'm holdin' it down, and I'm running low on product. You gotta put me down with your main connect."

I could tell he had something other than business on his mind. "No, what yo' ass need to do, is stop fuckin' with that nigga Stix." *How in the hell did he know that?* I lowered my head.

"Look, Kim, you ain't supposed to be sleepin' with the enemy. I told you long ago, this is not a game."

"I thought you two were cool. You said so yourself."

"I yell at that nigga to keep my enemies close." He nodded at one of the inmates walking by. "Don't fuckin' mess up my operation on some ol' love shit. Once bitches start gettin' poked, your emotions eat the hell away at your brain cells. Love has no place in the drug game." He grabbed my face. "Business and pleasure go together like oil and water. They don't fuckin' mix. Ya follow me?."

Tears welled up in my eyes. But I was determined not to cry. I was a warrior now. So I had to act like one. I couldn't believe he was telling me not to mess with the man, I care so deeply for. "Let's talk business," I said attempting to change the conversation.

"Pack yo' shit and find another place to live," he said, noticing my rebellion.

I took one long deep breath. "Look Bink, I need some product and fast. Where can I get it?"

He locked his eyes on me. "You don't wanna know."

"Bink, stop fuckin' playin' with me. I'm in this all the way. It's my life and I'm not gonna lose out for nobody."

"Don't get cocky, Kim. I made you.

"Who is it," I asked raising my voice.

"You ain't gonna stop until your feelings get hurt, are you?" I sat there waiting for his answer. He paused. "Big

Mike . . . it's Big Mike. He's my supplier. Is that truth enough for ya?"

"Fuck you Bink!" I got up from the table in a rage. He grabbed my arm and yanked me close to him.

"Just fall back, Kim. I'll be outta here shortly. Let me handle the big stuff."

"I got this Bink. I'm gonna handle my business, but it won't be with my no good ass father." I moved closer in his face. "I got this. I know what I'm doing."

He pushed my face away from his. "Just remember, the student is *never* wiser than the teacher." I bit down on my lip, snatched away from his grip, and stood up. He hopped up quickly, and grabbed hold of my ear. "You got all my paper ready for me, right?"

"Of course I do," I said yanking away from his grip."

"Keep in touch. I'll be out soon."

"Until then," I said sarcastically. "Don't drop the soap."

***

Chapter 18

I was starting to learn that nothing was consistent in life. Today, I became the proud owner of a 1990- 300 series BMW. White hooked it all up, and Stix helped me foot the bill. It was a birthday present for my eighteenth birthday. He even drove me down to take my driver's license test that I aced, only after a few days of studying. Even more inconsistent than that, was the fact that Big Mike wanted to meet with me to call a truce. I couldn't figure out if it was a personal truce or a business one. Through the grapevine, I'd heard that he said some real nasty shit about me. But it didn't bother me, 'cause the money was pouring in.

I sat in Mr. Jack's store for the first time with my father as the new owner of the store. Big Mike sipped his coffee, and crossed his legs slowly, never taking his eye off me. We sat face-to-face exchanging dirty looks, when it hit me that I was sitting in a dangerous situation. My father's shirt was pulled up just enough for me to see his gun peek through his baggy jeans. What he didn't know was that I had mine too. Who would have thought my life would come down to this.

"So why did you ask me to come here?" I blurted out, becoming impatient.

"We obviously need to talk," he said firmly.

I shrugged my shoulders. "Let's hear it, 'cause I gotta jet in a minute."

"Oh, so you gotta run to make, huh?"

His comment caught me off guard. But the games were getting old. "Look, we both know what game we're in. And I do mean *we.*" I looked at him closely making sure he understood that I had him figured out. "Let's cut to the chase," I said.

My father threw his hands up in the air, like he had a burning question in mind. "Kim, I ain't 'bout to loose what I worked hard for, all because of you!" He spoke like he was talking to a nigga in the streets.

I stayed calm. "How am I responsible for making you loose anything?"

"You serving my people! And you making me look bad in the streets."

"Your people sweating me." My hands moved like a seasoned gangsta. "I ain't calling them!" I could feel the nigga slowly coming out of me, as I rolled my neck in a quick circular motion.

Big Mike moved a little closer to me, looked me square in the eye, and pointed two fingers close enough to damage my eye-ball. "I've been in this business a long time." He nodded confidently while gritting his teeth. "And I refuse to be broke because you took all of my customers!"

"Binky's customers!" I shot back.

"He works for me!"

"It's about time you admit it."

"You got me," he said calmly.

I was starting to think Big Mike was bi-polar the way he changed his attitude in the middle of our family feud. He stood up impressed by the way he was getting' handled.

"Kim, you know I love you, right?"

"Oh, sure," I answered sarcastically.

"Your dad got himself into a little bit of trouble," he said popping open a bottle of E&J. "I need your help."

What kinda help would he need from me? And why is he refering to himself in the third person? "What you need?" I asked.

Small beads of sweat appeared on his forehead. "I got this one customer that needs some coke. I'm completely out, but this client is important. If I don't get my hands on some powder, I could be in a lot of trouble."

Big Mike poured two shots and took'em straight to the head. He seemed to be stressed. I definitely didn't want to help him, but he made it seem like if he didn't produce some product, he might make the six o'clock news tonight.

"Why can't you get more from your connect?"

He laughed. "Binky never paid me what's owed to me. He's locked up for now. So, until he gets out, I can't pay my connection for our past bill."

"Umgh." I hoped my father could tell I wasn't the least bit concerned. I spoke clearly when I said, "You prepared to pay me?"

He smirked. "Oh you gon' deal directly with the client. Think of it this way," he said, pouring another drink. "You'll be helping me, and making yourself some money at the same time."

Even though I had reservations, this meeting needed to be over. "Where he be at?" I asked.

"It's a *she* and she's ready to meet you."

"How much she need?"

"A quarter of a kilo," he said thankfully.

I stood from my chair ready to go. "Tell her to meet me across from White's at seven sharp tonight. That's six thousand," I motioned with my hands. "If her money is short, it's a no-go." *And it ain't my problem sucka, if she don't come correct.*

It felt good thinking those thoughts about my father, without him hearing it. I really wanted to say, *your day is done . . . and it's time for you to get somewhere and sit your old ass down. Let me show you how it's really supposed to happen.*

Instead, I headed toward the door with a funny feeling eating at my heart. I stopped dead in my tracks. "How long have you been dealing with this lady?"

Big Mike looked flustered. "Let's just say she's a close friend."

"Give it to me straight, or I ain't doing it."

He knew I was serious. "Kim, it's actually Ms. Donna Jack. Let's just say, I owe her big time. You do want your father to keep this store, don't you?"

This was getting to be way too much. Before I could say anything else, Tee-Tee appeared behind me. You could tell from the look on her face that she'd been standing there for a minute. As soon as she got within inches from my father, he pulled her close for a slight hug. Tee-Tee gave a fake smile. "It's good to see you Kim," she said. "Call me sometimes." She handed me a piece of paper with her number scribbled on it, that also read *don't do it.*

I thought, *they're both twisted.* While most fathers and daughters hugged before parting ways, instead- we gave each other dap. I headed out the door yelling, "Tell 'er to be on time, seven sharp."

I looked back over my shoulder one last time, when my dad shouted my name, "Kim!"

"Yeah."

"You got game, baby girl."

***

It was already five o'clock and time was running out. I had showered, collected a little money, and was a third of the way down route seventeen. I had already decided that once I replenished my product, I had to find a closer spot to keep my shit. It was bad enough having to travel so far out to pick up product, but coming alone was the pits. Black Tye had been actin' real shady lately, not answering my calls and shit. So I figured I'd keep him away for a minute. A broke nigga generally starts acting right when they down to their last dollar.

Pulling up within a half mile from the barn, I checked to make sure I hadn't been followed. Before getting out the car, I grabbed the brown tote bag from behind the seat. Even though Donna only wanted a quarter, my plan was to take the last three kilo's now, so I didn't have to come back out here.

Strangely, I wasn't scared this time. I strolled right up to the door of the barn, and flicked my flashlight on. Making my way to the chest, I was proud of myself. I was really doing this on my own. When I opened the chest, and lifted the duffle bag, I noticed that it felt light. Quickly, I unzipped the bag, and moved my hand from side to side.

I thought I was trippin'. Nothing was there! I hyperventilated for a second, then dropped the bag. I started to check the inside of the chest, or the surrounding area. Then I thought about it. Who was I fooling? Black Tye got me!

I moved in slow motion for a second as I thought about how I would kill him. *I wish I had the strength to gut him slowly. A traitor deserves just that!*

***

I had so much to take care of, but out of courtesy to my father, I decided to meet Donna anyway. I figured, I'd just explain to her that I ran out of coke, and that she'd be the first person on my list to get some. This way, maybe whatever deal my father had with her, wouldn't go sour.

I pulled up across the street from White's at about three minutes to seven. Just like Binky, I had become anal about time. As I waited for Donna, visions of me blastin' Black Tye entered my mind. I hoped that I could go through with it.

At this point, I had to make a statement. Then my people would know, not to fuck with me. I glanced at the clock on my dash, noticing that it was five after seven. Just as I was ready to pull off, I made eye contact with a woman who looked slightly familiar. Not sure where she came from, I watched her closely. She stood behind a Buick Sable like she was waiting for the right moment to walk over to me. Although average looking, she was a sharp dresser. I figured it was Donna, but couldn't be sure.

I had seen Donna at the funeral, but the black sheer

across her face kept me from really getting a good look. Instantly, a weird feeling shot through my veins. As the woman walked toward me, the multi-colored thigh high boots took me for a loop. I tried to calm myself, thinking, *this can't be the same woman who wore the red wig a few months ago*? Before I could get my thoughts together, the woman knocked on the window of the BMW.

Hesitantly, I rolled it down. "Hi, Kim," she said warmly. "I haven't seen you since you were little," she said.

"I've seen you," I replied.

"Oh, yeah. At the funeral, I was a mess. Don't really remember anyone," she said.

"Listen, Donna. I don't have anything at the moment. But I know someone who does."

Her face knotted up real quick. "I want yo stuff. I heard it was the best on the streets."

"Actually, it's not mine," I said, careful with my words. "I'm helping out a friend. I don't touch nothing though. I just make things happen."

Donna frowned. "That's not what I heard." I could tell she wasn't pleased. "When can you get something?" she asked.

"Be back here, tomorrow. Same time, same place." Before Donna could respond, I pulled off. I drove down to the end of the block and whipped a u-turn. With Donna still in site, I parked up on the curb, grabbed one of Stix's crazy looking hats from the back seat, and hopped out. I walked back toward Whites, hoping to see where Donna was going. Instantly, my eyes caught a glimpse of her as she pulled from an alley, driving an old 1980 blue Bonneville. *A mothafuckin'* undercover *cop*! I screamed inside.

***

Chapter 19

I was doing 80 down the beltline, headed to meet Stix. My problems had escalated big time over the last few hours. Black Tye jacked me for the last of the coke; I was being set up by an undercover cop, and had no idea who I could get more product from! One thing was for sure. I'd do whatever it took to stay on top. My customers loved me, they had become loyal to me, and I had to find a way to provide them with what they needed.

I wasn't about to become broke again, or share a jail cell with Binky's ass. Donna Jack had no idea that she was playin' with fire, about to get burnt. Now, while I never actually shot at anybody other than Ray-Ray, my hands itched. At that moment, I could visualize Donna Jack's brains sprawled out on the ground. One bullet to the head, and she'd be done.

When I pulled up to the Waffle House, Stix was waiting for me right out front. Today, he looked slick. His dreads were fresh, and dangled from the new toboggan, given as a gift from me.

I jumped out, and ran toward him, like I hadn't seen him in years. While I hadn't told him much over the phone, he knew I needed him by the sound of my voice. Stix's embrace told me that he'd be there for me. I felt like I could cry on his shoulder, but couldn't. Some strange type of hardness had developed in me.

"What me baby so upset 'bout?"

I didn't know where to start. So, I figured Donna would be perfect. I stepped back, looked him in the eye, and spilled my guts. "It all started when my father asked me to come to the store." It hit me, that for the first time I had referred to Big Mike as my father in front of Stix's. Scared of his reaction, I took another step back.

"Me know already," he said. "Whatchu hiding it for, star?" he asked.

"I knew you wanted to get him, and I didn't want it to affect our relationship."

"Star, yuh me womun. Nobody cum between us!" He hesitated. "As a matter of fact, I left 'em alone because he yuh blood."

"Not anymore," I replied. He tried to set me up!"

Stix went off. "Yuh blood clot punk," Stix yelled. At first I thought he was talking about me! "Yuh father must pay gurl. How he try tuh set yuh up?" he questioned.

"He asked me to meet Ms. Donna, and serve her some coke for him. He claimed that he was in big trouble because I had taken all of his customers."

Before I could finish, Stix was shaking his head back and forth. "I shoulda told yuh about Donna, long ago," he said. "The bitch tis a unda cover, dirty cop."

My jaw dropped.

"Donna buys cocaine, sells cocaine, sets people up, steals money, and kills!"

"Kills?" I asked in shock.

"Yuh Ms. Donna poisoned 'er husband 'cause he wouldn't tell 'er where the money was. She owed over $100,000 from deals gone bad."

I rubbed my temples as I took in all the information. *Cop or no cop, Donna needed to be taken care of.*

"Stix, worse than all of this . . . ." Black Tye stole the kilos I had set aside, and he's got most of Binky's money." I pressed my head against his chest. "I gotta get some product!"

"Don't worry pretty lady. Yuh come up wit' thirty thousand. That'll get yuh started again. Me have yuh product within a day or so."

I smiled. I knew that between the money hidden at my mother's house and money on the streets, I'd come up with the cash. I kissed Stix with every inch of my tongue. "Thanks for helping me."

"No problem. Me cook some for yuh too. Yuh gotta step up yuh game."

That's just what I was thinking. *We moving on to bigger and better things.* I slobbed Stix one last time, then heading out to round up my money. I had many things to take care of, including getting Rhonda ready to meet Ms. Donna.

***

A few days had gone by, and Stix and I were puttin' in work. The delivery came in, and my first job was to have Rhonda meet Ms. Donna. Rhonda had been stressing me out about giving her some work. But after I found out that she had my money stolen, I wasn't letting her make a dollar. Sam came out and told me that Rhonda paid some guys to do the job, and got nothing out of it. That made me realize, she just didn't want me to have nothin'.

Then, to add insult to injury, she told everything she knew about me to the police when they came snooping around. I had just about had enough of Rhonda.

I put on my counterfeit voice, and called her, to review the plan.

She answered like she was hyped, "Let's do this," she said in a high pitched voice.

"You ready?" I asked.

"More ready than I ever will be. You know Kim, I've

been thinking, me and you can run this town."

I almost choked. "Oh yeah?"

That's right. All you need is someone loyal on your team." I almost cringed when Rhonda said, "I'd do anything for you. You my girl."

She made that shit sound so believable that I almost told her not to show up for the run.

***

Forty minutes later, I sat in a rental car roughly fifty yards from the meeting spot. Patiently, I waited for Rhonda to hit the block. Donna was already in place; I guess waiting to make the sale. I had already made out a male undercover, parked a few blocks up the street, in a Ford pick-up truck.

While the under-covers thought they were slick, they didn't have shit on my disguise. With my short-styled wig, oversized sun-shades, and unattractive dress, I made sure my presence would go un-noticed. Stix knew all about the plan, and had my bail money ready if necessary.

I wasn't sure if it was the thought of jail, seeing Rhonda coming down the street, or if it was noticing the pick-up, that had me slightly nervous. For what I didn't know, 'cause Rhonda was the one who carried a quarter of a kilo inside her Fendi back-pack.

The view through my binoculars was great. Rhonda

strutted real sassy-like, shaking Donna's hand. As she walked up to Donna to deliver her package, everything seems to look so cool. Donna took the bag slowly out of Rhonda's hand, and swung it by her side. It seemed like she was shaking a bomb, because out of nowhere, the police came from all over. Look like they were even running from the DMV parking lot.

Donna immediately looked at Rhonda, letting her know she'd been made. The police were on Rhonda like flies on shit. People were getting out of all the cars, looking around like the biggest dealer in Raleigh was getting busted. I watched everything carefully to see what anybody's next move would be.

Donna finally cuffed Rhonda and read her rights. I wondered how many of the cops on the scene would be sharing in the coke they just seized. I'm sure, not just Donna.

***

Chapter 20

Life continued to move fast for me. Over the next month, I increased my paper, to the tune of some 60gs, and my relationship with Stix had become much more serious. So serious in fact, that we were now basically partners. He worked his Jamaican customers, while I worked my folks. In between sales, we lay on his waterbed and fuck ourselves to death. *Good dick and money, I am definitely on top.*

Being with Stix's had its benefits. For one, I had grown accustomed to watching and learning more about his deals. He even had me cooking up coke so often, I was damn near a chemist. The percentage rose from 80% to 90%.

I had been buying coke from Stix's connect over the past few weeks. Most of it, I cooked into crack, except for my clients who insisted on powder.

Stix spoiled me rotten. From daily shopping sprees to fine dining, I never wore the same thing twice. Oh, and you best to believe we ate like the rich and famous. Stix even hired a private cook to come sometimes to the crib, to prepare authentic Jamaican cuisine, as the chef called it. I wasn't used to spicy food. *My ass set on the toilet many of nights burning,* but I got used to it real quick.

One thing about Jamaicans in the states, they are particular about their girl's hair. I guess where he's from, and all the nappy heads they've seen, Stix wasn't having it. He sent me to the hairdresser every week. *Shit, I had too, because that nigga was constantly sweatin' my damn hair out during sex.* Today, I was really in need of a fresh do, so I showered, put on my gear, and rolled over to see my girl at the salon.

As soon as I entered the salon doors, I was greeted by the receptionist. "Welcome to Magic Fingers. Whose you're appointment with? Sign in and have a seat."

Damn, this bitch sure is perky for 10am in the morning. It ain't even noon. She must be trying to get the employee of the year award or some shit. As I proceeded back to the shampoo bowl, I could tell all eyes were on me. My thick herringbone chain draped across my neck, tennis outfit, slouched socks, high top Reeboks, bamboo earrings with Stix written in diamonds, and my Gucci purse were the envy of every trick in the shop. *I'ma really give em something to look at with my deep finger waves and french roll.*

You could always find out any and everything at the beauty salon. *These bitches run their mouths like water running down the Grand Canyon.* As Peaches styled and put the finishing touches on my hair, she spun me around in the chair and said, "You know Ms. Faye is a snitch. She would sell out her own momma for a workin' fifty. So watch your ass and your backside".

I couldn't believe what Peaches told me. "Not Ms. Faye. She might rat you out in the hood, but she damn sure ain't workin for the pigs".

"Gurl, you betta stop bein naive, ain't no luv in the streets. People know you makin' money. Maybe miss Faye feel like you owe her somethin'."

"I don't owe nobody shit!" Peaches' comment rubbed me the wrong way, 'cause I knew how hard I'd worked to get this far in the game.

"You know the word is Big Mike ain't too happy wit' yo' ass either. He done put a hit out on you." Peaches looked at me with a *you better believe it* look.

"A hit?" I laughed it off, as I grabbed my keys to leave the shop. *Damn could this shit be true? Fuck that shit, I can't let these rumors get to me.* Admiring my hair, I slipped Peaches a $100 bill, gave the shampoo girl a $20, and strutted out, giving all the gossipers something else to run their damn mouths about.

***

I pulled on the strip to see if I could get some info on

where Black Tye had been hiding. Stix had advised me to lay low for a couple of weeks. He said, "Give it sum time, yuh snake will sho." *I am going to kill his bitch ass, and let the rest of these mothafuckas know I ain't the one to take over a 100g's of shit from.* When I hopped out my Beamer and headed towards the young bucks chillin' on the playground, I noticed that scank ass Zandy walking through the cut. Reaching in my Gucci bag, I grabbed my 9mm and walked up behind her.

I snatched her pontail like she was a rag doll. "Bitch, I'm fixing to rock your ass to sleep, if you don't tell me where that punk ass man of yours is." I shoved the gun in her side to let her know this shit was not a joke.

"Kim I'on know where he is. I haven't seen or talked to him in a week." She was shaking like a leaf on a tree. "I don't have anything to do with what he did to you. I told him to just leave it alone." Tears streamed down her face and I could see the fear in her eyes. *I am glad this singing ass bitch ain't on my team.* "You treated him better then Binky did, and that was some foul shit he pulled."

"Bitch, you think I'm stupid." I cocked the gun and put it to her head. "Please Kim don't kill me. I will help you set 'em up if you want, just don't take my life." She pleaded with snot running down her face. "He is acting crazy as shit now, I don't know what's gotten into him. Look what he did to me!" She pulled up her shirt exposing the red and purple bruises on her body.

Damn I knew his ass was crazy, but that's crazy. "That's

your fault for letting niggas beat up on you."

"I got two broken ribs all because I questioned him about some skeezer he had in the car with him." She lowered her head and started balling. "I'm trapped. He said I'm down wit' him forever."

For a quick second I felt sorry for her, because I knew she really loved this nigga. "If you play with me, I swear to you, I will kill your whole family." I got so close to her face, that she could smell the double mint on my breath. "Here's my new pager number, so hit me when you get in touch with him." I released her hair, put the safety on the gun, and shoved it back in my purse. Watching her walk away, I laughed and said, "Zandy, don't fuck with me." She didn't respond. The buckling in her knees let me know my job here was done.

***

Two days later, I got a page from a number I didn't recognize. I wondered who the fuck it was. I hoped it was about some money or some information on where I might find Black Tye. After running into Zandy, and scaring the shit out of her, I had some of my other connects looking out for information on his whereabouts. He damn sure is doing a good job staying undercover, but when his ass does surface, he better have my shit, or its lights out. Just for fucking with me, it might be sweet dreams anyway.

"Yeah, who dis?" I spoke into the pay phone.

"Kim, it's Zandy. Tye called me last night. I didn't tell him that you were looking for him."

This bitch must want this mothafucka dealt wit'.

"He's supposed to call and hook up with me later on tonight.".

"Aight, cool. When he hits you back, see if you can get some information on his whereabouts, a place to meet up wit 'em, and call me back. Whatever you do, you'd better not let him know that I'm looking for him or there will be hell to pay."

I could hear the trembling in her voice, not to mention the fact that she was pronouncing her words like she had just started learning *Hooked on Phonics.* Zandy knew I meant business and for her own sake, she knew she needed to cooperate, or there was sure to be a front page news story about a family execution. *Family of four found dead at their home in east Raleigh, North Carolina. All four were found gagged and tied with multiple gun shot wounds to the head. The family dog had even been executed and was found hanging from a rope in his doghouse. More details on the 11o'clock news.* I smiled as I slammed the phone down in her ear. *That's some sick shit,* I thought. Like Binky said, *everyone is disposable.*

***

Staying on top of my business was priority for me, I had been out all day making runs when my new, huge cellular phone rung. "Hey Star, what yuh doin'?"

"Nothing much, just doin' my thing. What's up with you?"

"Me need yuh to meet me at home for a sample of that good stuff."

What the fuck is going on, this nigga is a nympho. Since we've been living together, he think the pussy is open 24-7 like the fuckin' convenience store. The shit is the bomb, but damn- a bitch gotta make this paper. "What's wrong Daddy you missin mama?" I teased. I turned on my sexy voice. "Big Daddy take my dip stick out and stroke it for mama." I couldn't believe Stix had turned me into a freak.

"Oh, me like it. It's hard for his mama," he moaned.

"Can you hold on until we hook up later?"

"Yeah, me have tuh be out late tunight. Me got business tuh handle." "That's cool, I got some shit to do too."

"See yuh later." He hung up the phone.

I got back in the car, and drove to the Heritage Park Projects on the south side of Raleigh. When my car rolled up, I spotted one of my workers walking with an elderly lady. He nodded his head to let me know he acknowledged me. He walked the lady in the house, returned to my car, and pulled out a black pouch. "It's all here", he said. *The one thing I learned is to keep the conversation to a minimum, 'cause it ain't much to talk about.*

I reached under the seat, pulled out a back pack, and handed him the bag. In return, he handed me a bundle of money from the pouch that I quickly threw in my MCM bag. *Damn a bitch needs to eat.* Driving to the Jamaican spot to get me some curry shrimp, and coco bread, I started thinking about what Peaches told me the other day. *Damn it's real fucked up my own damn daddy wants to take me out. He better know he got a war on his hands.*

It's amazing how my life has changed in the last couple of months. I got over 50g stacked, driving a beamer, got mad rags and jewels, and mad respect. I wish my momma would understand, and let me help her out. If her ass thinks she too damn grand for some help then so be it.

***

Zandy was starting to get on my nerves. Once again, I called her back. "Yeah, what's up?"

"Kim, Tye said he want me to meet him around 9 o'clock at his room at the Embassy Suites in Durham."

"I'll meet you in the lobby by the ice machine. Don't forget the key card." "Aight, see you at ten," she said, hanging up the phone. I called Chanel being as thou she lived near the Embassy Suites. To my surprise she was home, so I rode over there and kicked it with her 'til it was time to put our plan in to action. *Chanel would flip if she knew the shit I'm 'bout to get into. I got to take this nigga out by any means necessary, even if those means include smoking his singing ass girlfriend too. Niggas definitely gotta learn not to fuck with me, and my paper. I guess this theiven, bitch-ass nigga gon' be the first to learn the lesson.*

Like clockwork, Zandy was standing by the ice machine with key card in hand. As I approached her, I noticed the look on her face. She really wanted this nigga dead. *I guess that's what happens to a woman when she gets tired of being someone's punching bag. If that were me, he would never have seen the light of day the next damn morning or at least his dick wouldn't, because I would have chopped that bitch off in his sleep.* We went over our plans once again for about 10 minutes, then our plan was ready for action.

I entered the room dressed in all black. Crawling on the floor, I ducked beside the nightstand. With a .357 in my waist, and my nine-millimeter in hand, I was ready to get my rambo on. Black Tye was so busy with Zandy's pussy in his face he didn't notice there were now three people in the party. The light from outside of the window peeked through the curtains. This was the first time I had seen my former worker in months. I reflected on how cool we once were. *I remembered the day I was on the pay phone and the way he watched me. Damn, Kim. what are you doing, is money this important? Hold on, this mothafucka done took my shit and ran off like shit is sweet. Why am I so divided? I had to grind to get back and this motherfucker is laid up here drinking Don. I looked on the nightstand and saw a Rolex with a diamond bezel, a thick ass gold link necklace and matching bracelet. I was willing to break him off.*

Shit, I paid his ass better than Binky and this is the mother fuckin' thanks I get. Fuck him! Reaching on the side of the night- stand I located his piece right where Zandy told me she would place it. *Damn a woman scorned ain't to be fucked with.*

I watched them get busy contemplating the entire time. As Tye flipped Zandy over to the doggy style position, and took his place on his knees, I eased from the side of the nightstand, and knocked him over the head with the butt of my gun. I flicked on the lights, and instructed Zandy to put on her clothes. "Handcuff this nigga to the chair, and stuff his mouth with his underwear, I yelled to Zandy. "Put these gloves on and wipe off everything in here that you touched." I thought she would be scared and shaky but to my surprise she was on point. Filling the bathroom trash can with cold water, she took the empty ice bucket, filled it with water and threw it in the Microwave for five minutes. I was ready to end his life. "Wake him up," I said to Zandy as I turned the television on. I wanted to make sure no one could hear what was going on in the room. "Wake the fuck up you grimy mothafucka!" I smacked the shit out of Tye, just like I'd seen Binky do.

I dumped the cold water on his head and watched as

he instantly regained conscience "Hey, Tye," I said calmly. That nigga looked like he saw a ghost. With a wide smile I asked, "So you like taken shit that don't belong to you, huh?"

Face full of fear he shook his head, as I continued to talk shit, and circle the chair with my nine in one hand, and his glock in the other. "Zandy,show this mothafucka what the deal is!" I spat like I was Scarface.

'Ding' was the sound of the microwave, letting us know the water had boiled. "Niggas that fuck with my shit is considered to be real hot," I stated as Zandy poured baby oil all over his face. "So since you want to be hot, I'ma show you what happens when niggas like you play with fire."

Zandy threw the hot water all over his face as we watched his face burn and blister. "Melt," I shouted in between my hysterical laughs.

He screamed in pain. Next thing we knew, he was shakin' like he had a seizure. We clowned his fake ass, as Zandy fucked him up just like he use to do her. As we cleaned up, there was not a pulse in his body. But I was still unsatisfied so I placed the silencer on the gun and dumped 5 shots to his skull and left him right on that Embassy Suites floor leaking. I watched as Zandy began to cry in guilt. "Bitch, shut the fuck up for you be next."

"I gotta get myself together." She sniffled.

"Yeah. Do that. Or, I will kill you, and who ever resembles your ass." I grabbed her raggedy hair, and forced the nine in her mouth.

"I'm fine," she said. "Let's clean up."

After we wiped everything down, I grabbed all his jewelry and we stepped out the door. When I got to the car, I blasted my NWA and felt no remorse about what I had done. It's official. I'm a real gangsta.

***

Chapter 21

I tried to calm myself down. I really needed to focus on the car that followed me, four car lengths behind. All the talk about Big Mike trying to get me had me paranoid over the last few days. *At this point, it might be true.*

I swung to my left, but the brown Mustang stayed in the center lane. I breathed heavily, before thinking about my next move. Just as I approached the light, I reached in my bag for my nine. My heart skipped a beat when I looked up.

A black Bonneville was right behind me. Before the light could change, I sped off, and hung a left, right in the middle of on-coming traffic. *Damn, I'm a bad bitch,* I thought.

I bragged on myself too soon, because the Bonneville

was on my tail again. My eyes zoomed in on the rear view mirror searching for the mustang; but it wasn't in sight. I decided I've have to bust a move, in order to ditch these niggas. If I had to kill them, I was ready.

I sped up to the next block and whipped a u-turn, into the gas station. With my hand on my nine, I was ready to blast me a mothafucka! My jaw dropped when I got a glimpse of the driver in the Bonneville. "Officer Rodriquez," I yelled inside my ride.

Quickly, I slipped the gun inside my bag. Rodriquez stepped out of the car, and I did too. I prayed he wouldn't search my car. Going to jail for a gun charge wouldn't be cool. "Well, well, well . . . . What do we have here," he said, walking toward me.

I gritted my teeth, as he got closer. "What's this chase all about?" I asked.

"It wasn't a chase, until you made it that way."

"I ain't no dummy," I snapped. "I saw the brown Mustang, when I first hit New Bern Avenue."

Rodriquez had a puzzling look on his face. "Mustang? That had nothing to do with us," he said. "Maybe that was one of the drug boys, or even your father," he smirked.

How in the hell did he know about that? I guess my expression revealed what I was thinking.

"Kim, I'm a detective. I know everything. We're watching you, and our informants are too." He smirked. "You know, you were a minor, when I came to your house." He folded his arms firmly. "You're eighteen now." He grinned.

I cut to the chase. "What do you want from me?"

Rodriquez headed back toward his car. He looked back over his shoulder. "How about, thirty to life?"

My heart felt like it had dropped down into the bottom of my shoe. I sat in my car, and cried like a baby, for the first time in months. My body rocked back and forth as I had flashbacks of my momma. I missed her so much. Everything that had been constant in my life was gone; Momma, Ms. Faye, Binky, and Chanel were all gone!

Stix had been traveling a lot lately settin' up shop in Virginia, so he wasn't near. Even though he had been good to me and would come if called, I needed some sense of family. The word *family* triggered something in me. I scrambled through my ashtray searching for the number Tee-Tee had given me. The small piece of paper had been crumbled from sitting so long, but the numbers could be read.

I grabbed my phone and called Tee-Tee for two reasons. One, she always greeted me cheerfully, and desired to create a relationship with me. And two, she might be able to give me some info on Big Mike. When a voice picked up on the line, I knew it was her.

"Hello," she answered, like she didn't have one problem in the world.

"Tee-Tee, it's me, Kim."

"Oh my God, I'm so glad you called! Are you okay?" she asked.

"I'm fine." I smiled knowing that she cared.

"I don't know what's gotten into Big Mike," she blurted out.

I cut her off. "Say no more. Can you meet me at the Rock-N-Reggae, off of Western Boulevard?"

"What time?" she asked without hesitation.

"Six thirty."

"I'll be there."

"Oh, and Tee-Tee," I said, before hanging up. "Be on time."

"Got you."

***

Hours later, I walked into the Rock-N-Reggae a few minutes early. My plan was to grab a plate of curry chicken before Tee-Tee arrived. Just as I finishing speaking to the regulars, I noticed Tee-Tee sitting at the far end of the bar. *Early*, I thought. *Now here's a girl who understands the importance of time.*

I stepped up to the bar, pulled the stool out directly next to Tee-Tee, and patted her on the arm. "Thanks for comin'," I said, like this was strictly business.

Tee-Tee reached out and hugged me. Instantly, I hugged her back. The moment was so strange. It was almost as if she'd been my sister all of my life. "Kim, this is bad," she cried.

"It's alright. Dry your tears," I instructed. "So what's he plannin'?"

"He's crazy! And I hate 'em!"

"Tee-Tee, don't mess up your relationship with him, over me. He doesn't feel good. Trust me."

"He messed that up a long time ago." Tee-Tee had stopped crying, but was still very upset. "My mother is doing twelve years for his ass. Do you think he even visits?"

"Your mother is locked up? Because of Big Mike?"

"Yep, his underhanded ass tricked her. She thought Big Mike was gonna step up to the plate and take responsibility for the kilos of coke found in our house. During her trial, he convinced her to keep her mouth shut, saying that the District Attorney didn't have enough evidence to convict her. You see what happened, don't you." Instantly, the tears flowed down Tee-Tee's face once again.

I didn't know what to say. I just pulled her close. Noticing the barmaid headed our way; I motioned with my hand for her to leave us alone.

Tee-Tee looked me square in the face. She dabbed her napkin to dry the tears. "He paid somebody to kill you!" she whispered.

Even though I figured he had stooped to that level, hearing from Tee-Tee threw me for a loop. I sat all the way back allowing my back to rest, and my mind to race. I had to take care of Big Mike. What am I thinking, *kill my own father*? I sat up quickly, and studied Tee-Tee's demeanor. "You wouldn't lie, would you?"

"Why would I lie, Kim? He's already made my life miserable."

"You always seem to be happy."

"That's fake. Yeah, I'm thankful for my grandma, but all the stuff Big Mike does for me doesn't make me happy. He's just trying to re-pay me for what he's done to my momma."

"How much more time she got?" I asked, feeling sorry for her.

"Two more years. Together, we gonna gut his ass when she gets out."

I smiled. "I've gotta plan. But we'll . . . ."

Just then, my eyes lit up. I couldn't believe the figure headed my way. His swagger hadn't changed, but his feelings for me obviously did. Binky walked with a hard thrust as if he was there to take me out. I checked for a gun, but saw nothing. Quickly, I clutched my bag, just in case he was strapped. I slid Tee-Tee my keys, preparing her. "You might need to make a break for it," I whispered. I didn't want her caught up in my mess.

Binky approached me with the look of death in his eyes. It didn't bother me, because I learned the ropes from him. He always taught me to me to handle mine, so I was ready for him. Word on the block was, that he'd come looking for me once he got out. I just didn't think the time would be now.

"What's up, Kim," he asked with a mean grimace on his face.

"You tell it!" I spoke like a real thug, acting like I was really in control of the situation.

He spoke from his heart. "I taught you everything you know, I asked you to take care of the business while I was on lock down, and this is what I get?"

"I took care of business the best I could."

" What in the fuck, got into you, while I was gone? You tryna take over, Kim?"

A few people noticed that our voices had gotten rowdy. So they paid close attention to our area. I had to show off. "Tryna? I have taken over, and ain't a damn thing you can do about it! Yeah, you gave me the opportunity. But I executed the plan, and better than you. You always told me to look out for myself, and that's what I did!"

I prayed that Binky still loved me enough not to pull out his piece, and gun my ass down right here at the bar. Without delay, he stuck his hands in his pocket slowly. I watched him closely, while going for my purse. He pulled out a piece of gum, and put the stick in his mouth. "You must not know who you fuckin' wit'."

"I do. You taught me well," I bragged.

"First of all, I trusted you, and depended on you to do the right thing, and look at you now! You got my paper?" he asked, in a no-nonsense tone.

His last statement shocked me. "Look, I'ma be

straight up. I can do a little somethin' for ya. But , your boy Black Tye fucked up a lot of your money."

Binky shook his head in disbelief. "Damn, I'on believe this bull-shit. You gotta take full responsibility for my money, not Tye," he roared. Have my mothafuckin' money rounded up, soon!

I remained silent. I nudged Tee-Tee, signaling her to leave. But she was determined to stay put.

"I'll take forty thousand, and we'll squash the rest. Call me at this number," he said handing me a piece of paper. "If I don't hear from you in a couple of days, I'll assume you tryin' to fuck me."

I nodded my head while in deep thought. As Binky walked off, I thought, *pay this nigga, yeah right?*

***

Tee-Tee and I talked for another hour or so, catching up on each other's lives. I wanted to smack myself for treating her so badly in the past. She reminded me of my father's mother, her positive attitude in all. But me, I was nothing like my grandmother.

Instead of sending Tee-Tee home in a cab, she followed me to the beamer. As soon as we shut the door, an image of a brown Mustang was seen from the corner of my eye. I tried to zoom in on the two faces, but couldn't make them out.

Thankfully, Stix had taught me to always back into a

space. I flipped the car in drive, and took off to the end of the lot. When I got to the end, Binky sat in a gold Tahoe truck. He didn't budge; he just sat chewing on his straw. I wasn't sure if he was part of the chain gang that had been sent to do me, but I wasn't waiting around to find out either.

I put the car into reverse and back up like a racecar driver. I looked over at Tee-Tee expecting her to be scared. *Nada.* Tee- Tee focused on the opposition. Once again, I found myself near the Mustang. I was about to drive up on the sidewalk in an attempt to make it out the parking lot. Suddenly, the smaller punk in the car leaned out the window with his Uzi in hand.

I panicked. The bullets pounded my car, one by one. I felt no pain. It seemed as if this was a movie. Thinking on my feet, I backed up again, but this time over the curb and the tall shrubs behind me. My momma must've been praying for me, because the beamer fit perfectly through the landscaping.

By the time I had made my escape, my muffler sounded as it scraped the ground. I expected my assailants to come chasing me from the other side, but the sound of the sirens, and the flashing lights in front of me, probably scared them away. *Suckas*, I thought. *Real niggas ride or die.*

***

Chapter 22

It felt so good to be back in Stix's arms again. With my body nestled between his legs, I was sho nuff in Heaven. For hours, we sat discussing moves he'd made up north. Stix ran down our plan for moving to Virginia before Christmas. I liked the sound of increased money, but I knew a move like that would lessen my chances of getting right with my momma.

Thinking of my momma sent me into la-la land. Stix's voice snapped me back to reality. "Yuh hear me, gurl?" he asked.

My face said that I didn't.

"Me say yuh have to set up the meetin'."

Oh shit, hear we go again, I thought. Ever since he's been back, Stix has been pressuring me to make some decisions about handling Big Mike, the police, and

Binky. I had already decided, *fuck Binky. He get's nothin'.* But the set-up Stix had in mind for Big Mike and Donna, was growing on me, more and more each day.

I didn't wanna become a hard-nosed killer, but I wasn't going out like no sucka either. Living good was addictive, and I giving that up wasn't up for discussion.

"Go on, call dem," Stix insisted.

"I will. I just wanna get my tone right first."

"Scared litte gurls, don't make it in this business." He shoved the phone in my face.

I dialed Big Mike's number, and told him that I came to my senses. We talked briefly about the money that Binky owed him, but couldn't pay, because I sold the coke. My father acted like he and I never had a beef at all, when I agreed to come past the store on Friday to pay-up. I told him to tell Donna that I had two free kilos' for her too. When my father asked why was I doing that. I lied, and said that she kept me from getting locked up. Big Mike was so happy; he didn't question my reasoning no more.

***

I sat in the car a block away from Mr. Jack's store, and watched as people went in and out. I had flashbacks of all the events that took place at that store from my childhood. *All the good things that Mr. Jack did for people and now look at it.* My thoughts were interrupted by the sound of my cellular phone ringing. "Yeah"

"You ready to do this?" my sister asked, in a concerned voice.

"Ready as I can be," I answered. *After all this time I can't believe Tee-Tee would be the one to help me get our sorry ass father.*

"Okay, I'm going in to make sure everything goes as planned. I will unlock the back door and you can enter in three minutes."

I sat there thinking of the day she and I got into that fight, and Big Mike came to the school on her behalf. "Kim! Are you listening to me?" She could tell I wasn't focused.

"Look, Kim, this is something that has to be done, It's your life or his!" *Damn, this shit must come natural; flows through our blood or something. She's madder than I am, and she was his favorite child.*

I straightened up. "Aight, three minutes, and after we're done, I'll meet you at the Jamaican spot."

"Got it."

Minutes later, I watched Tee-Tee enter the store. Just as I was about to crack my door to hop out, I looked in the rear view mirror, and noticed Ms. Faye getting out of a Bonneville. I ducked down in my seat, and watched the two white agents ride pass me. Ms. Faye circled the block and went into the store as Tee- Tee was leaving out. I watched her bolt and lock the front door of the store. "Oh shit," I shouted. "Ms. Faye is inside." I reached under the seat and grabbed my nine with the silencer. *What the hell, I guess you get what you deserve in life.* On the side of the store, I picked up the propane tank that had been placed near the dumpster the night before. Entering through the back door, I could hear Big Mike talking to Ms. Faye. "Mike come on, give me a hit. I heard you keep plenty of shit up in here."

"Bitch, I'm out! I'm grinding hard, trying to get back on track."

I know she ain't wearing a wire. Big Mike is more stupid than I thought. Placing the portable gas tank near the boiler, I could hear Ms. Donna finally speak. *"You think she's coming?" she asked.*

Standing in the doorway of the office wearing an all black cat suit, a hoodie, and a baseball cap, I cleared my throat. Pointing the nine-millimeter at Donna, I dared her with my eyes to reach for her gun. Ms. Faye was already high, and didn't say a word. I guess guilt had gotten the best of her. Big Mike was confused, and felt he needed to speak. "Kim, we've been waitin' for you." He fumbled trying to get in the desk drawer where he kept his piece.

"Yeah, I know." I looked at him with disgust in my eyes.

"Looking for this?" Tee-Tee said, appearing from the front. She stood beside me, twirling his gun on her middle finger. He couldn't believe his precious Tee Tee was in on this. Sadness covered his face.

"Yeah sis, that's exactly what he was looking for," I spat.

Big Mike burst out laughing, "Oh so now you two are like Thelma and Louise?"

I didn't answer. I removed the Pepsi bottle from the front pocket of my hoodie, stuffed the rag in the bottle, and poured the lighter fluid inside. "Nope, we the daughters of a sorry piece of shit like yourself," Tee-Tee finally responded.

"Tee-Tee, I've always been a good daddy to you." He paused and took two steps towards Ms. Donna.

"Mothafucka, don't take another step. If anybody makes a move, get ready to get blasted!" I had the coldest look he had ever seen.

Tee-Tee and I both backed our way toward the back door, with our victims held at gunpoint. "You fucked up when you put a hit out on my sister." She paused and looked him in the eyes.

Right before we left, I had one last comment for Michael Reynolds. "You didn't think I would let you force me out did you." I giggled, lit the end of the rag, and tossed it to Mike. "See you in hell!" I turned the lock on the out side of the office door and slammed it shut. We could smell the fire and hear them banging on the door begging to get out. *Thank goodness, Stix had told Tee-Tee to cut the phone lines.* Leaving out the back door, I turned the knob on the propane tank. I could here it leaking as we walked away.

***

Standing in the Jamaican restaurant, Tee-Tee and I waited for our order. We noticed a crowd forming in front of the T.V. I walked over to see what was going on. "Eight people injured and two casualties in a gas explosion; no names have been released," the news reporter announced. "We are two blocks from where the explosion happened. Six adults and two children suffered burns and smoke inhalation after a gas propane tank erupted. It appears that the portable gas tank was inside the neighbor store owned by Michael Reynolds, a suspected drug kingpin." When I looked at the screen they flashed a picture of a pile of ruble. The building was completely gone, burned to the ground. *Damn I didn't mean for anyone else to get hurt.* A since of sadness came over me when I saw Mr. Jack's store gone.

I continued to watch the live coverage with intensity. "Here we are live – talking with James Simms, Raleigh's fire chief. Mr. Simms . . ." he put the microphone to the chief's mouth for him to talk. "Were there any survivors inside?"

"Not inside," he answered sadly. "But, firefighters treated the injured before ambulance crews arrived. Eight people have been transported to several local hospitals to be treated."

Tee-Tee had a strange look on her face as we watched the end of the report. "You know Kim, they said it's not known what caused the tank to explode." She giggled a bit. "It wasn't from a main supply, natural gas line. It appears it was a leak in the tank that caused the explosion. At least they don't suspect foul play."

I whispered to Tee-Tee. "What are you getting at?"

"Big Mike told me, I was the beneficiary on the store policy." She shrugged her shoulders. "Since it burned down, I guess we'll have to use the check from the insurance company to buy us another store."

I gave Tee-Tee a bear hug. We turned to leave the store when a black revolver pointed at my temple. "You got my money, Kim?" the guy wearing the ski mask asked.

I wanted to faint. Instead, I just closed my eyes.

***

Life Changing Books Order Form

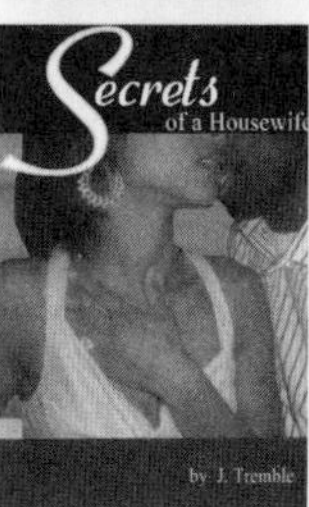

Add $3.95 for shipping. Total of $18.95 per book. For orders being shipped directly to prisons Life Changing Books deducts 25%. Cost are as follows, $11.25 plus shipping for a total of $15.20.

Make money order payable to Life Changing Books. Only certified or government issued checks.

Send to:
Life Changing Books/Orders P.O. Box 423
Brandywine, MD 20613

Purchaser Information

Name ________________________________

Register #________________________________
(Applies if incarcerated)

Address________________________________

City________________________________

State/Zip________________________________

Which Books ____________________________

# of books ______________

Total enclosed $___________

Nvision Publishing Order Form

Add $3.95 for shipping via U.S. Priority Mail. Total of $18.95 per book. For orders being shipped directly to prisons, Nvision Publishing deducts 25%. Cost are as follows, $11.25 plus shipping for a total of $15.20.

Make money order payable to Nvision Publishing. Only certified or government issued checks.

Send to:
Life Changing Books/Orders P.O. Box 423
Brandywine, MD 20613

Purchaser Information

Name ______________________________

Register #______________________________
(Applies if incarcerated)

Address______________________________

City______________________________

State/Zip______________________________

Which Books ______________________________

# of books ______________

Total enclosed $___________